The Shadow of the Dark

The Chronicles of Randy Carter Book 1

Sonya Lawson

SauceBox Press

Contents

Note to Reader (CW)

This book contains scenes that may depict, mention, or discuss assault, attempted murder, blood, cults, death, kidnapping, murder, occult, and/or violence. Please take care of yourself as you read.

To all my Columbus friends. You made the city shine
for me.

ONE

MY VAN SCREECHED TO a halt, rocking forward in a strong lurch as the wild rabbit continued to race across the narrow, wooded lane. It was a close call, for sure. Didn't need to plaster my white van with rabbit blood as I was dropping off a delivery. "Shit," I muttered to myself, hoping the red velvet cupcakes were safe in the back. Any order of five dozen wasn't huge in the grand scheme of things, but I didn't want to flake on a new client. Or clean up a mess of cream cheese frosting from the back of the van.

I eased off the brake and gently pressed forward, following the lane with the dim illumination of my headlights. It was weirdly quiet and dark here. Even if Upper Arlington was a little greener and more suburban, it was in the middle of the city and close to the university. Columbus didn't get a lot of thought when people considered major US cities, but it was densely populated and hustling for a landlocked Midwestern metropolis—mostly thanks to The Ohio State University's main campus. "The" is important there;

people get real upset if you don't include it. Something like sixty thousand students rested only a few miles from where I eased down this road. A large amount of people, even if you didn't include all the faculty and staff who worked there at all hours of the day and night. I shouldn't've experienced the sense of isolation and seclusion. I still did.

The secluded part and surrounding land were also definitely different, not like the open expanses of farmland surrounding Columbus, or the rolling green lawns of the large, expensive houses I was passing on my way here. It wasn't even an address, technically. The client, whom I'd never even met, had given GPS coordinates with their order, which should have made me pause. The order was so easy, and I was hoping to expand my delivery-and-special-event business more this year, so I hadn't even thought about it. Something supremely stupid, I realized with hindsight as I gripped the steering wheel tight.

There I was, creeping down what looked like a long and winding driveway, nearly blind because I had no streetlights to guide me and no real idea what would be at the end of the road. I was to leave the cupcakes and cookies, five dozen of each, in some type of wooden shelter. No set up. No contact. Only drop off and leave. Thinking about it made me more and more uneasy and unsure, but in for a penny, in for a pound, as some people somewhere used to say, I guess.

After a few more minutes of tense anticipation, I crested a small hill and found a large wooden shelter nestled at the base of a deeper ravine. A steep descent had me sending good vibes back to my cupcakes once again, in the hope I packed them well enough to stay secure.

After I finally parked, I heaved out a breath and let the tension I didn't realize I was holding slip from my shoulders. Out and around, I studied the cupcakes when I opened the back doors of my van. Nestled tightly and still unfazed in their box. Yay for that. The cookies were for sure fine in their boxes, as I had stacked them tight and secure early, so they fit into two small paper bags with my Warm Regards logo stamped on the front. Seeing the logo always made me smile, for so many reasons.

My business was doing well, more than well, really, but I was still new to this. I wanted more clients—more loyal clients. Hence my agreement to make this quick, easy, and slightly odd online order and drop it off in this weird no-man's-land in Columbus.

Out in the middle of nowhere, with no client in sight—not that I knew what this client looked like—there was no need to be in too much of a rush. I made several trips, carrying cupcake boxes one at a time, with the cookies looped on my arms during the last haul. I stacked them as instructed on the large rough-hewn table off to the side of the outdoor shelter.

The rustic shelter was beautifully made. Large beams worn with time rose from concrete, with a few dotted in the middle to support the massive roof. The wooden beams spanning the hollow interior of the roof looked intricately carved, with deep gouges shadowing the recesses. It was too dark to see what they depicted, the swirls and lines only barely visible in the deepening night, with only the small light from singular bulbs scattered around the shelter on cords so they swayed slightly in the late-spring breeze. In fact, it was beautiful but creepy, and it became more so as I finished placing my baked goodies on the side table.

Looking around for a moment to survey the scene, a sense of unease stole over me, like I was being watched. I stretched up on tiptoes to peek into the murky blackness of the night, but visibility was scarce. From the low vantage point, I spotted a dark building not too far away. Right on top of the shelter, in fact—another mark on the weird meter because it took so long for me to notice it looming there. Shrouded in total darkness before, the half-moon peeked out from the night clouds—so often scattered about during springtime in Ohio—and shone down on what looked like another building on the opposite end of the ravine. The dark structure towered over the shelter, somehow blacker and darker than the surrounding night, almost like a shadow reaching into the sky, with what looked like a steeple reaching upward. It was a small but high church painted in the deepest black. I shivered and a sense of dread, from the vision in front of me or from the general spooky atmosphere of this place, lodged itself in my throat.

I was about to leave, sufficiently creeped out and in no mood to wait around for a client I did not know, when a roar filled the air. No small woodland creature made such a noise, even if it wasn't exactly frightening. The sound hit a sadder note. It was a miserable, trapped sound coming from the direction of the big, black church building in the distance. The sound, as loud and out of place and potentially scary as it was, made my heart hurt for some reason. Pulled on my pity. I almost moved toward it, but I stopped myself, drawing up short and giving myself a shake to clear my head. All too much, and too affective for my liking. The dread and sense of danger were enough to make my steps back to the van swift and sure—until I froze, because right on the periphery of the shelter, people appeared. A mass of people dressed in dark, hooded robes.

It was a shock, watching what looked like several dozen people come out of nowhere to surround me as a weird roar echoed in the night. A few turned directly toward me as I hovered midstep on my way out of the shelter.

A giggle, so creepy and hollow it sounded more terrifying than the roar from before, rang out in the darkness at the other side of the shelter. Only twenty feet separated me from the figures closing in, obviously moving toward me with some intention I couldn't imagine would be good. Suddenly, from my back, powerful hands grabbed me from behind. I looked up and saw a blank, masculine face half-hidden by a hood. This all spelled not-good things for me, so I thrashed and bucked, trying to free myself. He held fast.

A saccharine-sweet feminine voice, which somehow lifted above the scream of danger ringing in my ears, gave out instructions. "Get the rope. Tie her to the beams."

Rope? Beams? It made no sense, none of it, but it was scary as hell. In the few seconds of frantic thrashing and disbelief, the man had moved me all the way to the other end of the shelter, past its bounds, closer to a tree line where I saw a patch of leveled dirt, several figures holding lit tiki torches, and a giant X half buried in the ground, made from the same thick beams as the shelter. As I got closer, I could see it had the same weird series of symbols.

I was being dragged there, and all I knew was it would not end well for me. There was no way a group of hooded figures dragging someone to a giant St. Andrew's cross buried in the ground could end well. My utter confusion and panic nearly took me under, but I somehow cleared my head, took a deep breath, and thought for a moment. More hooded figures moved, forming a circle around what I assumed was my final destination. The man slowed enough to let others get into place for something, as if waiting for everyone to gather before he pushed me into the sea of hoods and onto whatever they had in store for me. His bruising grip ached, but it was only a grip on my arms.

Realizing I needed to get free or risk some horrors I didn't want to know about, I stopped blindly thrashing and reared my head back to headbutt him. A loud, resonating thud sounded. Pain blossomed across my skull, but I had to ignore it. I turned in his loosened grip and kneed him in the balls, which made him drop like a bag of flour before I stumbled away.

My head pounded and my instincts screamed, so I bolted, heading full steam back to my van at a speedy clip, much to the surprise of the robed figure staring after me. I could run faster than most people thought I could, but that was their own bias getting in their way. People underestimated chubby girls like me all the time, and right then, I used it to my advantage. I heard the roar sound again, as if calling to me or spurring me on.

A high-pitched female voice with a soft twang called, "Stop her. Now."

A handful of hooded figures chased after me, torch-light slipping into the inky night behind me, and I knew there was only one thing I could do. I hadn't done it in ages, but the power pulled on my gut, urging me to use it, to dip back into the neglected well. So I slipped into the shadows, like I had so often when I was young, like I'd sworn I'd never do again after my horrible night out with Merry and Mia during the tornado.

Two

ONE THING 99.9 PERCENT of people who knew me do not know: I had this weird superpower. It wasn't something immediately handy, like telekinesis or mind-reading or flight. It was a little like teleportation, just not as cool. Was why one of my favorite X-Men had always been Nightcrawler, but that fun fact about me wasn't exactly important.

Instead of being able to poof out and poof back in at a different location instantly, I could kinda move into a strange, shadowy version of our world. I pop into a place where everything is the same, but it was all gray scale, like an old black-and-white movie. Time seemed to run the same, objects were the same, and people were still there. The difference was the people couldn't see me, but I could see them. I could then move around like I normally would without being seen.

It might've been useful, if it weren't for the downside, which was admittedly huge. There were other things, the creepy and scary things, living in the grayish world I visited.

First, there were living shadows that crawled all over me. I could feel them move and slide across my skin. When I was little, it'd been funny. Amusing. The older I got, the more scared I became about those things latching onto me, because I didn't know what they were or what they wanted. Kids didn't question motives, but when I'd started thinking about it, the more frightening possibilities crowded my thoughts, and I couldn't shake the feeling they wanted something from me. Something I might not be willing to give.

Second, there were monsters there. I mean honest-to-God ripped-straight-from-childhood-nightmares type monsters. They'd started showing up if I stayed too long, as if my being there attracted them. If I was in the shadow world for, say, five minutes, I'd hear them. It was a slide and slither of wetting things, or the stomp of massive feet. I'd feel them coming as if I had a sixth sense for them closing in on me. I'd even seen eyes in the deeper shadows of the space, but only glimpses. I'd never confronted one of the things, never even got a close look at one until much later in life. My body would get clammy, and my nerves would start tingling, my version of Spidey senses. I'd dip out real quick when the feeling became overwhelming, luckily before anything serious found me. Except for the last time... hence me not wanting to go back there. Ever.

I'd been able to slip into this other place, whatever it is, for as long as I could remember. I had apparently started doing it as a toddler, which had sent my parents into multiple fits. They'd refused to believe my stories about the shadowy place until one day, I'd winked out right in front of their eyes and came back moments later, giggling and talking about creepy crawlies on my skin.

To say my normal-ass, working-class Midwestern parents freaked out would be an understatement. They weren't religious, but they'd started talking to people who were in broad hypotheticals. When they got no answers, they read up all they could on odd phenomena similar to this. Mom and Dad found nothing. They'd tried; they really had. The story of their life with all the Carter sisters, really. They always tried, no matter what, and we loved them fiercely for it.

The other Carters didn't have any type of super-powers, unless the patience my parents had shown while raising three stubborn-as-hell daughters count-ed, which it should've. My younger sisters were special in their own ways, but no superpowers there either. At least none had manifested. It was only me in my family with this odd tic, and my parents hadn't found anything to help any of us understand it.

When I had been little, it hadn't mattered. I'd played in the shadow world by myself sometimes, messing with my sisters or parents while I'd scampered around unseen. The older I got, the scarier the place seemed. Real life was a big and scary place on its own. Add another version only I and some menacing creatures inhabited, and it had felt like I'd needed to stick to what I knew and what I—and everyone else around me—understood.

There were times I'd slipped in during my late teens, like when I was being sexually harassed by this asshole at a party once, but mostly I steered clear. The last time I'd slipped through was on Merry's twenty-seventh birthday, and it hadn't been a choice—it was out of fear. I regretted it for many reasons since, one being I'd caught sight of one of the slithering things and nope. Just nope. It was too terrifying to talk about, too terrifying for me to actually talk for a while after I'd blinked back to reality, in fact. Freaked Merry and Mia way out, even more than the tornado that had jumpstarted the whole horrifying chain of events.

Afterward, I'd sworn I'd never do it again. I'd stay where I was, firmly planted in the real world. But I figured when I had menacing robed figures outside a looming black church in the middle of nowhere threatening to tie me to a cross, it might've been okay to break a promise to myself.

Luckily for me, the shadowy world was more gray than black at night. It made my path away from those creeps brighter and easier to navigate. While they stumbled around in the darkness, their torches illuminating a small circle around them, I booked it toward my van as fast as I could. My thighs chafed and my legs strained as I ran toward my goal on the opposite side of a shelter. I ignored the shadows clinging to me and caressing my skin as if they had missed me as I pushed forward.

Curiosity got the better of me, however, and I slowed enough to look behind me. Their robes were dark gray in the shadows and spotted with strange glowing symbols. I'd never seen anything like it. Whatever they had written on their clothes was reacting in this world somehow. If they weren't chasing me in the dark, I might have stopped to question them about it. As it was, I didn't think they'd be too friendly at the moment, so it was likely best for me to not know.

They didn't appear to have their own superpowers, stumbling as they ran blindly in the dark in different directions. Two robed figures searched side-by-side, somewhat organized but still ineffective. They couldn't see me hidden in my shadow world, so they searched for someone no longer there. It would be a hilarious game of Marco Polo on dry land, if it wasn't because they wanted to kidnap me for some reason I knew had to be nefarious. As if any form of kidnapping wasn't nefarious.

One pair was stumbling in my direction, but the darkness made them slower and more careful, which gave me plenty of distance. Didn't last long, because a lone figure in a fully shimmering robe stepped out from the pack of people still circling the beams embedded in the ground. She threw her hood back. I saw her face clearly, what with the glow of symbols flowing up her neck flaring bright for a few seconds. She was a petite, light-haired, fair-skinned, button-nosed young woman. Could be any smiling and cheerful OSU sorority girl I saw on the daily in my café, the ones who too often got a bad rap because the world didn't like to let women enjoy things. The hard slant of her mouth and the hateful crinkle of her steady stare marred her pretty-girl looks. Her stare, oddly enough, was pinned right on me. As if she could see me.

Which apparently, she could, because she screamed out with her harsh twang, "She's right there, you idiots! Heading to her van." She looked right into my eyes and cocked her head when I jolted in surprise. The hard line of her mouth turned into a sickeningly sweet smile when she yelled to me, "Seems like we got a lot to talk about, honey," as her minions headed in the direction of her pointing finger.

There was no time like the present to get my ass out of there, so I stopped my snooping and booked it. Sadly, there were some great runners in the hooded-figure game, and a few were getting a little too close for comfort. I'd have to slip back into the real world to get into my van and get away, and at this rate, they'd be right on top of me when I did.

I gasped and pushed myself harder, running for all my might from the robed figures and the monstrous sounds I heard in the shadowy distance. I knew I'd have to jump back out before those things jumped me, no matter if the humans were close. No matter if I hated the idea.

I was hoping against hope, running full tilt, but they were gaining. Until I had yet another surprise. A figure slipped into the shadow world in front of me, several yards ahead, closer to my van. I wouldn't have believed it if I didn't literally watch the space shimmer before a person emerged, solid and tangible in the world of shadows. They were lean, dressed in all black, and had a black hoodie pulled up. They pushed it back, and I saw her face—a face I had seen earlier in my café, staring at Merry. My sister had stared back, smitten at first sight, which was why I remembered her now. She'd also been sitting with the tall hunk of a man who'd camped out in my café during the last two weeks for at least an hour every afternoon.

I stopped, shocked at her appearance in a place I'd never seen another person before. Her hands and arms glowed with the symbols, like the robes. She yelled out harshly, "Damn it, run! I can buy you a little time."

I kept running, moving past her, close enough to feel her presence, to hear her muttering things under her breath. Her hands glowed brighter as I stared over my shoulder. I felt a wall of something invisible rush out from her palms, air shimmering as it had when she came through to me, heading out into the real world to knock all the robed figures I could see to the ground.

She turned without a second look and yelled, "Come on!" as she zipped past me. Also a better runner apparently. I saw the big hunk of a man from my café bouncing on the balls of his feet as if ready for a fight.

He sported a few of his own glowing symbols on his dark clothes and the tattoos on his forearms. We were less than ten feet from my escape when the woman muttered words and blinked out of the shadows, back into reality. I shook my head in disbelief again but pulled on the feeling deep in my gut to follow her out, and I stumbled to a stop in front of my van.

"Get in the vehicle," she barked.

"My vehicle, you mean?" I snapped back. "Who said you were invited?"

"We don't have time for this. Look." She pointed past me, back at the figures now peeling themselves off the ground. Any moment they'd be up and running, literally. She was right. I had no time to quibble. They seemed to be helpful, at least right now. I'd sort out everything else later.

The big guy wrenched my driver's side door open. For a second, I thought he was getting in, but he smiled back at me and waved me inside. A gentleman even in a crisis, apparently.

I dove in, not bothering with my seatbelt for the moment, and cranked it on. The woman was already in the passenger seat. The man climbed in through the back doors, which I didn't even wait for him to close. I floored it, bumping up the hill and over the lane toward the exit without turning on my headlights. I flipped the beams before turning onto the small side street that would eventually lead me to the lights of Columbus, away from this weird night. Questions spun around in my mind.

"What the hell?" was the one I yelled first.

The woman beside me laughed, but it was mirthless. Then she grimaced, the flash of white teeth stark against the night and her dark-brown skin. "Was going to say the same damn thing," she muttered.

Not helpful. Not at all. At least the dude in the back was mindful once again. "We'll explain, Miranda. Promise. Just get us to the café."

I didn't even question how he knew my name. I'd never talked to him, much less told him my name. Whatever. There was a lot I didn't know. The name bit seemed inconsequential as the van screeched onto Lane Avenue and headed toward Warm Regards.

THREE

IT WAS THE DEAD of night as I drove silently through the streets of Columbus, careening as fast as I could toward my café. I was on autopilot, turning on the familiar roads, moving from Upper Arlington to the campus area into the familiar grounds of the Old North neighborhood.

Old North was an odd place, which was why I liked it so much. Nestled between The Ohio State University's massive campus and the hipster haven known as the Clintonville neighborhood, the small strip of neighborhood was a mishmash of student-centric businesses jammed into older brick buildings dotted with the occasional gas station or fast-food restaurant. High Street, the main thoroughfare running through the bulk of Columbus, bisected the area, with many businesses planted along the busy street. There were small shops, cool eating spots, and lots of bars, which made sense with it being so close to a college campus and all. Surprisingly, there weren't many cafés, and no bakery cafés. Made it the perfect place to start my small business years ago, after my life had kinda fallen apart. Although, I'm thankful for all the falling apart now.

Like most women in their early thirties, there was a lot I did and did not do in my life. After pastry school, I'd landed a good job at the Greater Columbus Convention Center, creating cute, tiny, flavorful desserts for meetings and conventions while I'd saved to open up my own place. It was supposed to be temporary, a quick one-year pit stop before I moved on to my thing.

Then he'd come along. Of course he had. There was always at least one of those "hes" in any story about a straight woman's life. Even though I had been in my early twenties when I'd run into him in a German Village bar, I'd never lacked in male attention. I was mid-sized, a little between plus and not, but I had enough tits and ass to make many men take notice. I was also not afraid of it, not deterred by my size. I was proud of my body, what it could do and what it could feel.

Back to him. His name was David. Three years older than my twenty-two, he was beautiful, smart, and very much into me. He came from New Jersey coastal money, moved to Ohio for Miami University, and stayed there through his MBA. Got a big job at Huntington Bank headquarters in Columbus out of grad school and was all set to make it his thing for life. He was engaging, sexy as hell, and ambitious.

I'd fallen hard and wanted to build a life with him. Don't get it twisted, I'd made those choices. I had to own that. David had encouraged my decision to stay on at the convention center rather than strike out on my own, and he'd talked often about the failure rates for food businesses, but ultimately, I had been the one who'd let myself believe him. In every way.

I was married by twenty-four, then divorced by twenty-nine. A nice young woman who came to me in tears ripped those love blinders off. She confessed she had slept with him for six months before finding out he was married. I started the divorce filings immediately. I liked to think of myself as a fiercely loyal person, but loyalty should only extend to those who showed it in return. There was a lot I could sacrifice for those I love, but loyalty was paramount for me. Someone showed major signs of disloyalty, I was done. Even if they were my husband.

I had thought a lot as David had fought me through the divorce. About how I'd given up pieces of myself over the years voluntarily. I knew then it was a blessing he'd cheated, because he was a man who would ask a woman to give up these things and be happy when her dreams died a slow death in service of his own. Again, I was not blameless in all this. Love could blind or be blind, and in the small moments where I had given pieces of my dreams away, I had been happy and willing to do so to build something else. The difference was my partner hadn't felt the same, and it wasn't until I stepped back out of love when I saw how much I'd put in for so little return over the years.

David got the house and the cars, the toys and status symbols he liked so much. I got the lion's share of the savings, enough to make my dream an immediate reality. Less than three months after my divorce, Warm Regards opened in the Old North neighborhood of Columbus, close enough to OSU to get some student business but far enough away to make it comfortable for my sanity as a newly divorced woman staring down her thirties.

My parents helped with creating the space, putting their literal sweat into the building I bought: the café space, kitchen, and the apartment above it. Merry, the middle Carter sister, was a genius with accounting, though she used it for good as she worked with a LGBTQ nonprofit in town. She started my financial systems and did my books. My little sister, Mia, was a computer whiz. She worked in web design and security, but she created a kickass digital logo for me and upped my social media game. Upped it so much, after three short years in business, I had been making more than enough to hire people to run the actual café so I could focus solely on baking for my walk-in customers and special-order clients.

I was lucky. I'd put a huge chunk down on buying the building that housed my business and my apartment. It was a square, two-story brick storefront built back in the 1950s. Modest but sturdy. A little like me, or at least I liked to think so. The first floor was the small-ish café space which led back into my massive, state-of-the-art kitchen. It was the love of my life, really—the place where I spent most of my time.

My apartment above was large and airy, a mostly open space with the one bedroom and bathroom closed off. A space perfect for hanging out with my sisters, cooking for my friends, living a solid life. The building, which I'd been in for three years, had seemed like home since I had first walked in, even before I'd bought the place.

I felt grounded there in a way that seemed right, which was probably why I didn't question it at first when the strange, tattooed dude who helped save me suggested we go there.

NONE OF THIS CALMED my nerves as I screeched the van to a halt in its reserved spot within the tiny three-car lot behind the building, barely avoiding a run-in with my Mini Cooper. I sat gripping the wheel so tight, my knuckles felt strained, and I stared unseeing at the back of the building. After a few moments, the woman next to me seemed to think it was okay to speak.

"Miranda –" she began with an exasperated sigh, but I was having none of it.

"Out. Now."

She started again. "Miranda, we really should dis-cuss—"

I turned to her slowly, the look on my face apparently enough to stop her speech while I took her in fully for the first time.

Even with her sitting in the van in dark, nonde-script clothing, I could tell she had a lean, honed body. Or maybe I just remembered it from seeing her be-fore. With her hood back, her close-cropped black hair sprung up in tiny, tight curls across her head. Her facial features were sharp, all cutting cheekbones and hard brow with a wide-set nose making a slash down the center of her face. Her mouth was full and lush, even if it held a look of annoyance. All of it made me very aware of how Merry could find this woman mesmeriz-ing after their simple encounter in the café earlier in the afternoon. However, with her sleeve pushed up to her elbows, I saw the faint outline of strange symbols embedded there, like tattoos on her skin created with barely legible ink.

"What are you?" I asked in a whisper.

"What am I?" she replied, her tone expressing clear offense at the question. Which, fair enough, if it wasn't for the circumstances.

"What am *I*?" I asked then, and my voice cracked when I did. My whole life, I'd known nothing about my powers, about this weird thing I could do. Now here was someone I literally saw do something similar. Do more, in fact. Maybe she could answer my question, the one always rattling around in my mind: why was I so different?

She let out a harsh breath, as if again annoyed, but gave me the best answer I'd ever gotten on the subject. "I do not know, but you clearly have magic—magic on par with my own, which took me decades to learn. You seem to come by it naturally."

The man in the back eased his head into the space between the seats. "If I may," he interjected, ever so politely. "Perhaps we should begin at the beginning. My name is Gareth Davis. This is Harley Warren. We are mages."

"Like magicians or sorcerers?"

"Close enough," Harley answered.

"Okay, so what was all that back there?"

Gareth looked me up and down, concern clearly coming through when he asked, "First, are you all right? Were you injured in any way?"

"Physically, I'm fine. In my head, I'm screaming, so..."

"At least you're smart enough to wig out right now," Harley mumbled. "Can we get out of the car, get inside? I don't enjoy being out in the open after what went down tonight."

I hesitated. I didn't want them in my space. I didn't know them. However, Harley had saved my ass. Gareth seemed very polite and gentlemanly, but I knew enough to be wary of it for a time. Plus, they'd already been in the café. They knew it was my place. I'd even brought them here without thinking.

I didn't answer. Instead, I shoved my door open and walked calmly to unlock the back entrance into my kitchen. The others followed suit, at least from the sound of it, but I didn't spare them a backward glance. I hurried into my space, into the comforting realm of bright white and gleaming stainless steel that greeted me when I flipped on the overhead light by the door.

Moving to the middle of the room, I leaned against my giant prep table, the cool steel a bit of solace I barely felt through the rough denim of my black skinny jeans. Eyeing the two figures as they made their way into the light of my kitchen, I jumped slightly when the door banged closed.

"Apologies," Gareth muttered, looking down at me with a soft smile. He had to look down on me because he was massive. I wasn't short by any means. I was a respectable five foot eight. He towered over me at least a good ten inches, standing more than a head above me. He was also big in terms of muscle mass. Not '80s-era-Arnold big, but obviously muscled and homed in all the proper places, filling out his dark clothes deliciously. His hair was tied back, a long, shaggy, thick dirty blond. The same shade of hair covered his face. A thick beard surrounded bowed and rosy lips. His hazel eyes, the color of old forest trails, stared down at me. They looked kind. Like his companion, his pushed-up sleeves revealed dark-black swirls of tattoos. He gave off biker vibes. His kind eyes and polite demeanor might not be what one would expect from a stereotypical biker. The hotness, though, was on point.

I had no time for it, however. I was in internal freak-out mode. Magic. I was magic. I knew it already, but hearing someone else confirm it, someone who I knew was like me, was making questions bubble up and race around my mind. I was having a hard time deciding where I wanted to start.

"Okay, first things first," I said aloud, though it was more to organize my own thoughts. "What happened tonight?"

"The Starry Wisdom Cult," Harley answered, stepping farther into the kitchen to lean on a counter across from me. Gareth hovered between us, his arms crossed and his feet firmly planted shoulder-width apart.

"Like, an actual cult? Devil worshippers or something?"

"Or something," Harley said.

"Unhelpful, Harley." Gareth turned toward me. "Starry Wisdom Cult is a cult Harley has followed for decades. They've been around over a hundred years at this point. They worship a particular Outer God."

"Outer God?" I was full of questions. All this was new and terrifying, and my mind raced, trying to keep up with both the events and information.

Harley answered this one. "Think ultra-powerful being from deep in the cosmos. Some think they even started the cosmos, and they could end it if they wished."

"Okay…" I hesitated. Gods were a little much to take in, but people being assholes felt familiar, so I latched onto it. "Is the cult dangerous?"

"Exceedingly so. Death, destruction, apocalypse. That's their whole bag," Harley replied.

"I just happened to deliver cupcakes to them?"

"Doubt it was a coincidence," Harley said, standing straight. "If the leader saw you before somewhere, she knew you had magic."

"What do you mean?"

"You're covered in shadows. In a way I've never seen."

I fidgeted, feeling slightly itchy, thinking of what I saw in the shadowy world. Were they there all the time, and I didn't know it?

"I'm magic, something you've never seen before. But, again, what exactly?"

Harley looked at me, her eyes thoughtful as they took in all of my being, studying me from a few angles with the tilt of her head. "I'm unsure, and there's not a lot I don't know in this business."

Gareth jumped in then. "Harley is a well-known mage. I've been training for a few years, but she's been at this for over four decades."

I snorted. "What, since you were a baby?"

"No, since I was in my twenties. I don't age like most people anymore." Harley rubbed her arm in an absent-mined way, but it brought my eye back to the light tattooing there.

"Is it because of those tattoos you have? Why are they different from his? Are they the same as the ones glowing on the cult people's robes?"

"You can see Harley's markings?" Gareth asked back, ignoring the other questions right then.

"Well, yeah. They're not as big and bold as yours, but I'm not blind. They're faint swirls all up her arms and down her hands."

"Most people can't see these sigils, Miranda," Harley said, holding up her hands to my face, "not unless they're mages or something else well-versed in magic."

I shrugged, because what was I supposed to say? I saw them. Put it as another weird mark on the list of my weird magic powers.

"We've established I'm weird or unknown or whatever. Moving on to the more practical. Are we safe here? Is my café safe?"

"No idea," Harley replied. "They ordered from you, right?" At my confirmation, she said, "Means they know about you and this place. They could come looking for you tonight, days from now, or never again. I don't know why they wanted to take you, so I can't be certain of anything they may or may not do to get you again."

"Not reassuring," I muttered, hugging myself a bit.

"Not meant to be reassuring, but honest," Harley said. All this magic nonsense scared me, and I didn't like what she said, but I appreciated her saying it that way, being straight with me.

I had few options. My parents had retired to Florida, so I wasn't driving all the way down there in the dead of night. I could go to Merry's or Mia's places, but I didn't want to risk bringing whatever this mess was to my sisters' doorsteps.

"Miranda," Gareth called, grabbing my attention.

"Randy," I muttered.

"What?" he asked with a smile.

"No one calls me Miranda. At least, no one who knows me. It's Randy. Randy Carter."

He bent his head in a small bow and softly said, "A pleasure to formally meet you, Randy Carter." Harley snorted from her spot against the counter, and I ignored her as Gareth continued. "I can put up a few wards, give you some level of protection while you're in this building."

"Will it keep them out?"

"Not indefinitely, if they're persistent, but certain sigils could give you enough time and warning to prepare to fight or run."

Harley looked me up and down before saying, "I'd run if I were you."

I bristled, squaring my shoulders and turning my chin up in the air. I thought I had done well, considering I had gone in blind to the middle of some dark cult meeting at a creepy black church and had a mage yelling at me in the shadowy realm from my childhood.

Gareth sighed and moved forward. He did so slowly, as if he was afraid to spook me. Made sense.

"I can place the wards outside, then you can rest. We'll chat more tomorrow when you have time to think through some things."

Harley nodded, also apparently done talking. I didn't know these people. Didn't know if they were good or bad, honest or dishonest, but the promise of a small piece of protection from the kidnapping cult sounded good.

I agreed and waved them on, firmly shooing them out of the kitchens and outside so I could take the staircase up to my apartment. Standing in my kitchen upstairs, I watched Gareth mutter and move his hands. A flash of shimmery light appeared for a moment, then dissipated before he moved around the building and out of sight. Harley was nowhere to be seen.

Not wanting to get caught watching him, I stepped away from the window and headed for my room. I didn't think I'd sleep much that night, but comfy pajamas were in order, even if sleep was unlikely.

Four

As EXPECTED, I SLEPT little. Luckily, I didn't need to get up early the next day to open the café. I'd prepped everything I needed to handle long before last night. With my assistant manager, Deb, and two employees scheduled to work, I lazed in bed, listening to the soft sounds of the bustling café below, muffled through the floorboards. Eventually, I dragged myself out of bed. A quick shower and I was downstairs grabbing a drip coffee and a day-old muffin before I started my day.

For the next few hours, I lost myself in baking. It was easy for me, as it was something I still loved. Baking was an important part of my success. My sister Mia's skills with Instagram turned my cool cupcake and pastry ideas into social media gold, so while many people in the neighborhood came in because we were a good spot to hang and do work while getting a coffee and a tasty treat, there were people who traveled to Warm Regards specifically for the type of baked goods I posted on my socials.

The bake I decided on for the day mimicked my dark mood. A cupcake spin on a black forest gâteau, it consisted of a deep, dark-chocolate cake, kirsch black-cherry filling, and a cherry-vanilla buttercream covered in dark-chocolate shavings. A candied cherry, sweetened and preserved to a nice maroon color, sat on the very top, giving the smallest shade of color to the racks of deep brown and frigid white treats. They weren't exactly a spring confection, which was what most were making during this season, but they matched my mood perfectly. And they were pretty damn tasty to boot.

As usual, I put in my headphones, pulled up my work playlist, and got lost in the driving industrial and darker EDM beats I liked when I was trying to tune out the rest of the world. The music and baking calmed me, allowed my mind to go blank for a time and focus on the physical task of creation and the movement my body made to the music.

When a hand grabbed me on my shoulder, I let out an ear-splitting scream. I spun around, expecting to fight off some demented cultist, and saw Merry and Mia staring at me with startled looks. Merry's lips were moving, but the pounding rhythm of Massive Attack drowned out her words.

"Huh?" I said as I ripped the earphones from my ears.

"I said, 'What's your deal?'" Merry repeated, slowly enunciating as she did.

"You're the one who grabbed me," I groused, side-stepping the question altogether.

"Because we've been standing here for a full minute, and you didn't notice," Merry said, concern now coloring her tone. She cocked her head, her forehead creased in thought, and asked, "What's wrong?"

Of the three Carter sisters, Meredith—known as Merry to all who loved her—was the most intuitive. Not in a magic-powers way, to be clear. It wasn't mind-reading or clairvoyance. She just knew people or cared about them a bit more than others, including myself, and she could always pinpoint when something was off with them. Particularly with me, as we were so close.

Mia, the youngest and furthest from me in age, was also the snarkiest of us, which was no mean feat, because I had plenty of sass to go around. "If you being dead to the world a minute ago wasn't enough of a clue, those massive bags under your eyes say something kept you up last night." She shoved her black-rimmed glasses up her nose and moved around me to snag a finished cupcake from my tray.

"Hey!" I yelled, trying to stop her thievery, but she easily skidded around me and put Merry between us.

"Don't worry," she called as she pulled out her phone. "I'll snap a few choice pics of it before I eat it."

"Fine then, brat," I said, but it lacked heat.

"You never answered my question." Merry folded her arms across her chest and stared at me. It might have been an attempt to look tough, but it fell flat. Merry was the epitome of the girl next door. A real Marianne—from her willowy, lithe frame to her lush, dark hair, to her big, light-brown doe eyes and pouty lips. She had the demeanor to back it up too; always caring for others. She was a real nurturer, our Merry. Every American man's stereotypical dream, if it wasn't for the fact she was a lesbian, something she'd proudly proclaimed to everyone in the family when she was ten years old.

Her care for others even extended to her job. She was an ace with numbers. A truly gifted accountant who knew all the best tactics, the ins and outs of tax law, investments, anything financial. She could work as a bigwig at any of the large corporations around the city, making lots of money. Instead, ever since she'd graduated from college, she'd worked at a small nonprofit that helped LGBTQ homeless youth in the Columbus area. The nonprofit, and those kids, loved her for it. They also loved my cookies, which I sent to their space weekly.

I rolled my eyes and answered, "Nothing. All good here."

"Yeah right," Mia muttered through a mouthful of cupcake, dark frosting smearing her full lips. "Damn, sis. This is really, really good."

"Everything I make is good," I huffed. "And you better—" I stopped there because the telltale whoosh of an incoming text matched the smile on her face and the twinkle in her eyes.

"Already did." She popped the rest in her mouth and gave a groan of satisfaction.

Whereas Merry was tall and willowy, and I was mid-sized with solid curves, Mia was short and full-on voluptuous, like a miniature Betty Boop. Unlike me and Merry, who gravitated toward longer hair styles, she kept the Carter sister trademark dark hair in a cute pixie cut which she meticulously styled every day, so it beautifully topped her lovely round face. The black glasses she'd worn over her light-brown eyes since she was a child added a hint of old-school cool. While I favored dark clothes and leather, and Merry preferred float dresses, Mia dressed like the computer geek she was—jeans, Chucks, and nerdy pop culture tees.

If someone lined us up side-by-side, it'd be clear we were sisters, but there were definite variations. We were different physically. Our personalities were also different. Didn't matter. They were my best friends, and I was theirs. It was us against the world, always had been, and while I wanted to strangle them sometimes, I also would die protecting them. Which was exactly why they didn't need to know what had kept me up last night.

"You're not good, Randy." Merry was pressing again. "What gives?"

"Nothing. I swear. Nothing new. Just a rough night. Couldn't sleep. There was a lot on my mind."

"Is business okay?" she asked with genuine concern.

"Yeah, but super hectic. Thinking I might need to hire more people out front. Maybe even someone back here."

"Is it stressing you out?" Mia asked flat out.

"Maybe a little." I knew they needed to latch onto something or they'd keep digging. "Must be nervous about the idea of hiring my first baking assistant, I guess."

"Oh, babe. You're aces. You know that." Mia pulled me into a hug before she hip-checked me with a laugh.

"Yes. You'll do great because your baking is great," Merry said, a dazzling smile in place. "Plus, you have us here. And Mom and Dad cheering you on from a distance. We'll all help however we can."

"You already do too much, without pay," I chided.

"You pay me in free cupcakes," Mia said.

"Not by choice," I countered.

"We don't need pay. You help us, we help you. It's how the Carters work."

For some reason, maybe the fear and stress of last night—or the fact what she said had always been true, despite the fact I was so different from the rest of my family—Merry's words choked me up a little. Tears dotted the corners of my eyes, and a lump lodged itself in my throat. It was enough to make me turn away, back to my worktable, to hide the swell of emotion from my sisters before they started asking questions yet again.

I cleared the emotion from my throat before I spoke again. "If you've got nothing better to do than interrogate me, how about you do it while you help? These need to be put in the chiller, the next batch needs to come out to cool, and there's icing to be piped."

They grumbled but got to work. Partially because they were used to their older sister bossing them around. Partially because, despite their grumblings, they loved me and wanted to do whatever they could to help.

MAYBE I NEEDED TO pray to one of those Outer Gods. Thank them for the fact Merry and Mia were long gone when someone pounded on my kitchen entry door. I was upstairs, trying to veg in front of some reality TV and eat the gooey grilled cheese and canned tomato soup I had made, a nod to my childhood I found comfort in well into adulthood. When those three hard hits to my sturdy metal door sounded, I peeked down from my upstairs window and saw Gareth and Harley looking right up at me. Gareth was grinning, open and friendly. Harley wore a blank expression I couldn't read.

I opened the window and yelled down, "I don't want any," hoping it would be enough to make them scatter. No luck there.

"We simply want to talk for a minute, Randy," Gareth yelled in his deep voice.

"What if I don't want to talk?" I asked.

Harley looked up and, without losing her blank expression, said, "I think you know we don't exactly need an invitation to enter. We need to talk. You need to listen. It's going to happen either way."

"Harley." Gareth sighed, his polite demeanor apparently affronted by Harley's honest answer. I didn't like what she'd said, or the implication the mages could come into my place any damn time they wished, but I liked bluntness. She wasn't hiding what she could or would do. I respected her level of direct conversation; I just didn't like the topic under discussion then.

After a long pause, I answered, "I'll be down in a moment." I could hear them out if it meant my kitchen door wasn't blown off its hinges or melted or erased from existence by some sort of magic attack from Harley. I could politely listen and then tell them to get bent. No problem.

The creak of the metal door sounded appropriately ominous when I slowly opened it. Harley stalked in, taking up the same spot she'd occupied last night. Leaning against the counter again, I took in her clothes: a soft blue-and-gray striped shirt buttoned all the way to the tippy-top, gray slacks, matching black leather belt, and wing-tip shoes. She was impressive, intimidating, and attractive all at once.

Gareth hovered behind me, waiting for me to enter the room. From the little I knew of him, he likely did this to be polite. Let ladies enter first and all that jazz. However, I was in no mood for politeness. I stood my ground, turning back toward him slightly and giving an exaggerated sweep of my arm to let him know I needed him to be in front of me, in my line of sight and away from the back door and the door to my apartment stairway so I could at least pretend I had an escape route.

After a few beats of silent stares all around, I sighed and said, "You're here. Say what you have to say so you can leave again."

Harley pushed up to stand straight and tall, a well-dressed slash in the uniform shine of my kitchen. "Straight to the point. I think you have a lot of questions. We can answer them. I can also help you with your abilities, powers, whatever you want to call it. I propose an alliance of sorts. You help us take down the cult. We give you training and information. Simple exchange."

"What if I don't want training or information? What if I want to be left alone to run my café and live my regular old, magic-free life?"

"I think you and I both know your life has never been regular or magic-free, no matter how much you wished it had been," Harley said. She wasn't harsh in tone, but she'd hit the nail right on its head with her comment, enough to make me turn more defensive.

"Look, lady. I don't know you or this dude here. I don't even know exactly what happened last night. All I have are stories you told me. No one's shown up at my door to drag me off to be sacrificed yet."

"They haven't yet, but they will," Gareth said, deep and low. "Please, Randy. Consider taking our help."

"I'm not much into taking candy from strangers," I said in response. "As of now, I have no reason to help you, although it seems to me, you coming here, you have some reason to get my help in all this mess."

"True. You're powerful—naturally powerful in a way I've never seen in my many decades in the occult world. But you don't know what you have, you don't know how to use it, and one day soon, some bad guy's going to show up at your door and take advantage of all those things you don't know. One already tried, and nearly succeeded, last night."

"How am I supposed to believe you're not another type of bad guy?"

"You're right to be hesitant..." Gareth said, but Harley shut him down with a shake of her head.

"If she wants to be stubborn, ignore what she saw last night, push aside all those questions she's probably got spinning around in her head, let her. I've got no time to drag someone into reality."

"What you're talking about isn't reality!" I screamed, frustrated with this conversation and the absolutely bizarre turn of events within the past twenty-four hours.

Harley moved quickly, grabbing me by the hand before I could stop her. She muttered words, her arm symbols glowed, and *poof*, we were suddenly in the shadow world together. It'd been a long while since I'd traveled there. Much longer since I'd been to it twice in such a brief span of time. One memory I never forgot, a rule I somehow knew as a child, was the slithering things in the dark gravitated toward fear and presence, and they stuck close after any trip—so close I could already hear them closing in on us within seconds of stepping into their world.

Harley didn't know this or didn't care. She muttered, "Wasn't even sure that would work, but thought it might, given your natural affinity toward shadows."

I breathed. "How did you do that? Why did you do that?"

"How? Sigils, magic, and years of training. I did it because you needed a dose of reality. This"—she gestured around the shadow world—"is no less real than your kitchen on our everyday plane of existence. It's a part of it—a part most can't see or interact with, true, but no less real."

I didn't want to hear, didn't want to believe, and didn't want to be back in this place so soon after running through it out by the black church. "We have to leave before they come for us," I said.

"The cultists? They aren't around, Randy. It looked like the leader could at least see into the shadow plane, but I doubted she could enter it. If she could, she would've done it when they were after you."

"No. Not the people. The slithering things. The wild beasts. The monsters who lurk here in the shadows."

"What monsters?" Harley asked, looking around.

"You can't hear them?" I already sensed the slow but determined march toward us, the sounds becoming clearer, nearer. Too near.

She shook her head. Her eyes got big for a moment before she glowed again, grabbed my hand more gently, and pulled me with her back to the harsh lighting in my workaday kitchen.

I was breathing hard, as if I'd run a marathon, but fear was causing the rapid rise and fall of my chest, as well as the hyperventilating over the terror I felt because of all this newness and the weight of knowing there were others at least somewhat like me in the world and they were using magic to fight bad guys out in the streets of Columbus, apparently.

"Out," I said once I caught my breath.

Gareth reached toward me. I figured he meant to comfort me, but I was having none of it.

"Don't touch me," I hissed, and he stumbled back, his eyes wide and his hands up in a placating manner. I saw it then, from my peripheral vision, a wisp of dark shadow flailing up like a flame from my shoulder. I whipped my head around and it was gone, but I'd seen it. Something too much like the shadows that crawled over me in the other place.

"What did you do to me?" I cried out, frantic, hitting my shoulder as if I could brush it away.

"Nothing," Harley answered calmly, "but remind you of who you are."

I was shaking, fear and anger warring inside me. "I don't want this. Don't want whatever it is you're offering. Get out of my kitchen, now."

"Suit yourself," Harley said, walking toward the door. Over her shoulder she called, "Don't come crying to me when something scarier than me or you shows up here one dark night."

She disappeared out the door, letting it slam behind her. I heard Gareth move close to me, but I stepped away. "You need to leave, too."

He simply nodded, giving me the space I needed without a parting shot at me. I locked the door behind him, staring at the slick blank metal for long minutes after I'd heard them leave.

I didn't know if what I had done was right or not. Didn't know if I was safe anymore. Or if I ever actually had been. Maybe I'd been living on borrowed time for thirty-odd years, and my bill had finally come due.

Five

I KNEW GARETH WASN'T letting it go when the following day, Deb, my kickass manager, came in the kitchen a little after noon to tell me some hot dude wanted to speak with me. I popped my headphones back in their case after finishing off my lemon sugar cookie dough and putting it in the fridge to rest. When I made my way to the front, I was not at all surprised to see Gareth sitting, mug of coffee in his giant hands, at one of the small tables near the front window.

"What can I help you with?" I asked plainly as I took the seat opposite him. I figured a dude like him, so pressed about being polite all the time, wouldn't cause a scene in my café, but I'd been wrong enough times to be more cautious and less caustic right off the bat.

He held his hands up in a sign of peace and said, "I wanted to talk to you one-on-one. Harley can be… blunt at times. She can also withhold information, especially if she doesn't know a person well. I figured if I talk with you, honestly and freely, you might be more inclined to accept her invitation."

"You thought interrupting my workday was the best way to go about this?"

"I apologize. I didn't want to show up alone, uninvited, late at night. I thought, of my options, this would be best."

I didn't want to like him or trust him. I didn't, exactly. Yet there was something about him. Gareth was hot, of course. He also had a calming presence. His aura or whatever, it soothed me when I was close to him. I'd felt it the few times we had interacted already. It took the familiar bustle of the café in the light of day to confirm it was real and not some quirk of the heightened emotions playing out in our other encounters. It was damn hard to not fall into the sensations headfirst with a big hunk of a man like Gareth, though I was trying my best.

He and Harley weren't exactly wrong, either. There was a lot they somehow knew about my abilities—much more than I knew, for sure. I needed answers. Had needed them my entire life, so I couldn't exactly turn down this offering from Gareth without possibly regretting it in the future. Didn't mean I had to agree to whatever he asked, but it meant I got to learn a bit more from him. All it would cost me was a conversation. Not too high a price from my position.

"Okay. Seems fair enough. Come on, then." I rose and headed toward the back. We didn't stay in the kitchen this time, however. Too many eyes and ears around in the afternoon. I took him back to my tiny office, a rarely used space in the back of the building. It was big enough for a desk, a filing cabinet, and two office chairs. When we got in and situated with the door closed, I had second thoughts about the location. Gareth's big-badass-biker-like frame and the wave of his presence, even if it was calming, overwhelmed me in the room. I braced myself as best I could and nodded for him to begin. I wasn't starting this conversation.

He let out a deep breath and locked eyes with me. "Last night, it seemed like you didn't know about the shadows around you."

I shivered in response, not wanting to dwell on the discovery for too long. "Nope."

"I've been coming here to the café consistently for a few weeks now. Your coffee is wonderful. Your baking is amazing. You yourself are lovely as well. However, the initial draw was the shadows around you. The first time I saw you, they were large, looming even. Ready to burst with power and possibility."

He hesitated for a moment, as if thinking about the best way to proceed. "Everyone has auras. What you have isn't that. It's a special type of shadow called by magic, bits of darkness some mages can see and sometimes manipulate if they have the proper training and affinity for this type of work. Like me and Harley, but we can only see them to use them. You, though. I knew you were no mage right away. There were no sigils, no outward sign you called all this power to yourself through spells or incantations. It clung to you for another reason. You're drenched in power, a natural form of magic and power emanating from you with no coaxing. You don't realize it, but you have magic dripping from your skin, causing this dark cloud to hover all around you."

"Doesn't sound good. Can I stop it?"

"Unlikely."

My face must have shown my fear and anxiety, because he reached a hand out to pat mine.

"At least the magic part. It appears to be part of who you are as a being. Take it away, and you are no longer Randy. It also seems connected to your ability to work in the shadow realm. That's high-level mage magics, something I can't do. In fact, Harley is the only person I know who can. At least was, until we saw you flit into the shadows the other night. No sigils, no spells, no burst of external power. You just walked right in like it was nothing. Quite impressive, actually."

"I don't want to be impressive," I said, annoyed by the awe he seemed to have for this power I'd always had and always worried about. "I don't want this power. Don't need it. Frankly, if you could drain it from me, I'd be thankful."

He shook his head sharply. "Don't say such things. Harley and I have done some research, but we've found nothing definitive. However, if the power is natural, it may intertwine with your life force. To take it could mean you would die. I suspect Starry Wisdom saw your power and thought to harness it for themselves.

Thought to take it without caring it could also mean taking your life."

I knew the cult wanted to hurt me. Hearing it spoken aloud in Gareth's calm voice was still jarring. "Okay, so no getting rid of it, and if anyone else tries to take it, it could mean death. Can I tame it somehow?"

"You can train it. Or, more aptly, train yourself to use it. It would help with the shadows clinging to you. I suspect they were so concentrated when I first met you because you hadn't spent your magic in a long time. It accumulated around you without release, calling the shadows to you without you even trying to do it. When you shifted, you used power without realizing you did so. The shadows around you were smaller, more contained and less dense. Even now, they grow. To tame them and your magic, you'll have to use them."

I thought back to the times I'd shifted between worlds as a kid and when I'd used it to help myself as a teenager. How I had sworn it off for years and then it had reared up and bit me in the ass the night the tornado hit. How, though I didn't like to admit it to myself, it had leaked out in odd ways here and there when I had been going through the emotional turmoil of my divorce. It was a part of me. Responded to my needs and fears, if either were great. A part I could use without thought, like a reflex. Many of Gareth's theories were reasonable. It could be a good thing to drain it with use, keep it calm by learning more about it. Maybe I wouldn't attract attention like the type I got from Gareth or whatever cultists stumbled upon me.

"Say I agree to you and Harley's deal. What exactly would it entail on my end? You'll teach me, train me to use magic so I can control whatever it is welling up from inside me, and you get what? A new weapon?"

He squirmed in his seat, clearly uncomfortable with the question. "The wording is harsh. You would not be a weapon, an inanimate object for our use. You would be a partner in our fight against Starry Wisdom."

"And why should I care?"

"Because they kidnap, maim, and murder. They use people without regard and throw them away like trash. Their ultimate goal isn't conducive to human existence."

"What is their goal?"

"To bring one of the Outer Gods to Earth, make our human plane of existence accessible to them so they can rule, wreak havoc... do whatever it is immortal and immensely powerful cosmic beings might want to do to any dimension."

"Basically end-of-the-world type stuff," I replied. When he silently agreed, I let my head fall back. The ceiling wasn't an interesting sight, but it allowed me a moment to think without looking at this pretty dude sitting inches away from me. If we were talking apocalyptic stuff, it was not something I could ignore and still be able to look myself in the mirror or look my family in the eye.

"I take it you have a plan to take down this shitty cult?"

Gareth perked, sitting up and leaning forward. "It's a hazy plan right now because there are too many new variables in play. Having you with us might give us more options and better odds as we gather more information."

"Okay. You teach me, I'll help."

"Sure. To be fully transparent, it would mostly be Harley teaching you, not me." When I stared back at him, he rushed to fill the silence. "I know she can be abrasive and blunt, but she's the best mage I've ever met, and she knows more about magic than any other person I've ever encountered. She'll be able to train you well. Much better than I can. However, I'm sure I'll help occasionally."

"Do you think I don't like Harley?" I asked, wondering why he was selling her so hard.

He shrugged, and I laughed.

"I have no problem with her. She's direct. I appreciate the approach most of the time. I've just been a little freaked out lately."

"Good." He grinned at me, and a dimple formed on his right cheek. He was too good looking for my own good.

"Okay, so I guess you've convinced me. I should go talk to Harley about all this too, though."

"Yes. You should." Gareth checked his phone for the time and said, "I don't know Harley's schedule, but

I do sometimes physically train with her, so I know she'll likely be at this small boxing gym in Grandview where we like to work out. She should be there later on this afternoon. It'd be a good place to chat with her on neutral ground."

I found the address on Google Maps. Seemed easy enough to find on my own. "Okay, so I should go there? Meet her without her knowing I'm coming?"

"Oh, she knows I'm speaking with you. She said it was idiotic, but she knows. It might surprise her a little, you showing up at her gym, but you won't really surprise her. And before I forget." He leaned to one side to pull a thin, palm-sized book out of his back pocket. "This is a primer on the Starry Wisdom Cult. I was going to give it to you regardless of what you decided. Either way, it's information you need to know, given the fact the cult is concerned with you."

"Concerned with me." I snorted. "What a nice way to put it. I'd say, 'lured me to a deserted area and planned to do unspeakable things to me' is more likely."

He didn't laugh. "A likely possibility, Randy," he said with a solemn shake of his head, causing a shiver of fear to trickle up my spine. All of this was real and was really serious, and I needed to learn more. I took the book with a small thank-you and slipped it into the side phone pocket of my leggings.

I rose to leave at the same time he did. It brought Gareth and me close, our bodies an inch from touching in the small space. My breathing hitched. The feeling

I got from him, of calm and peace, intensified, though lust also grew in the background.

"Excuse me," he said, his voice even gruffer than normal.

"No worries. It's a small office. After you."

He didn't immediately turn to leave, but stayed inches from me, staring down from his height, studying my face.

"I... uh... yes. I should be going."

"Yup," I said with a sly grin. Gareth liked me, or at the very least found me attractive, and the big hunk was nervous about it. It was adorable. If there wasn't shadow and darkness and cult members circling around, it would be something I'd want to explore immediately. Sadly, the calm and physical sizzle swirling between us would have to wait, at least for a little while.

He stumbled out and gave his overly polite goodbyes, leaving out the back kitchen door. I returned to work. I could make lemon sugar cookies in my sleep, which was good, because my mind was not on cookies. It was mostly on Outer Gods and shadow magic and cult danger. Occasionally, though not too often, it may have also been on cute dimples and large hands.

Six

THE GYM, WHICH WAS actually a boxing club of sorts, was in a squat brick building among one of the many small business clusters lining Grandview Ave. Between a pita sandwich shop and a furniture restoration spot, it was easy to miss. There were obviously no bells and whistles at this gym. All it seemed to offer were the basics. A few cardio and weight stations stood mostly empty, with punching bags and small matted areas dotted around a fighting ring. It was all I could see when I opened the door. After a Beat I noticed a small hallway at the back, which I assumed housed locker rooms and an office of some type. As a small business owner, I knew an office was necessary. Business created a lot of paperwork, physical and digital, and it had to go somewhere. Plus, it was always good to have a private space for chats and whatnot. My talk with Gareth earlier was a prime example.

As soon as my eyes adjusted to the slightly dimmed lighting of the interior, I realized the gym dudes noticed me before I fully registered them. Most people had stopped what they were doing to look my way. The two men in the ring beating the absolute crap out of each other, and the coaches yelling at them both, were too busy. Everyone else had stopped and was staring.

I didn't know if it was because I was a woman or a newb. In a gym, it could be either. I didn't have time to question it, however, because from a far corner, I heard Harley's matter-of-fact tone rise above the noise of two men punching each other in the face.

"She's looking for me."

At her call, everyone seemed to go about their business, and I made my way to the place where I heard Harley. She came into sight halfway around the ring, a dark blur in a dark corner. She was wailing on a punching bag, causing it to swing freely with each punch she drilled into the bag.

It looked painful. Visible in her long sleeveless shirt, Harley's tense muscles bunched in anticipation, then sprang into action when the bag finished its small arc away from her from the last swing and countered back, rushing toward her again. Her tape-wrapped fists hit the bag with a dull thud. It was hard enough to shake her arm and send the bag reeling back to start the cycle all over again.

"Aren't you supposed to have somebody holding the bag for you?" I asked.

She grunted in reply, catching the bag to stop its inertia. She heaved deep breaths in and out, moving quietly to a bench along the wall. When she sat and started unwinding the tape from her hands, she motioned with her head for me to take the space next to her.

"I like to do things on my own sometimes," she answered, staring at her hands.

"Same," I mumbled, a little unsure where we were supposed to start and how to even begin with what we needed to do.

"I take it Gareth's 'friendly discussion' went well?" she asked, still not looking up at me, engrossed in the tape on her hands.

"Yeah. He's a real gentleman, that one."

"Yep. And it's not an act." She looked up when I scoffed, and she gave me a slow smile. "I know, hard to believe, right? A big good-old-boy-looking white man like him, not being an asshole on some level? Unheard of. I've known him a while now. He hasn't shown assholish tendencies yet. Though, his desire to play peacemaker and hero is an issue all its own."

"As much as I appreciate the character rundown of your friend, I'm not here to talk about him."

"Didn't figure you were. Just making idle conversation." She balled the tape up and threw it in a perfect arc into a trash can a few feet away. Leaning back so her shoulders hit the concrete wall behind us, she turned her head toward me and gave me the up-and-down. "You want to join us?"

"Want isn't the right word. More like I need to."

"That's no lie," she replied, turning her head to look at the ceiling. "Gareth told you a lot. Likely told you some about me too. Not much, because he doesn't have too much to tell, but enough, I suppose." She straightened and turned her knees toward me, facing me fully so she could look me in the eye.

"As a general rule, I don't mince words, and I don't coddle. I'm not some benevolent magical teacher out to save you, and I'm never going to sacrifice myself for you. I have my own shit to deal with, like you and everyone else. As of now, our goals align. We can have an exchange. I help you get more control of this magic you have, and you help me take down this cult we both need taken down. No more, no less."

"Sounds fair enough. Like I told Gareth, I'm not scared of you being straightforward with me. Hell, I prefer it. With you, I know what I'm getting."

She nodded, looking from my eyes to above my forehead for a moment before saying, "Your shadows agree."

"How can you see them?" I felt weirdly exposed by the fact she and Gareth and some of those cult creeps could see something on or around me I couldn't.

Harley pulled her shirt up slightly, exposing a small section of abdomen, and pointed at a faintly glowing mark there. "See this?" she asked. When I confirmed I could, she continued. "It's a sigil most mages or occultists get early on, if they're going to do any kind of magical work. It allows you to see how magic manifests in or around a person, if the person holds magics. You seem to have the ability already, because you can see the signals on me and Gareth. You saw some on those Starry Wisdom shits."

"Would this mark help me see magic better?"

"It should, but working on connecting with your magical ability might make it unnecessary. Like a muscle, you build up magical power with repetitive use. You do practice, you might see magic better than even I can with this ink."

I considered what she said. I needed practice, and quick. I felt like a marathon runner who didn't know they were even in a race until the competition was already miles ahead.

"How long will it take to get my magic mojo up to par?"

"Can't exactly say. It's all dependent, like most things in life. We can start and gauge where you are, how your magic works. After seeing more, I'll be able to give you a better idea." She hesitated for a second. "I have to be straight with you. I've never worked with a person with natural magical abilities. There's affinity, sure. Gareth and I both have inherent ability to varying degrees, as do most mages and occultists. Natural magic is a whole other beast, one I don't fully understand. I can't say what I do to train mages will help you or not. I can say I'll give you all the info I have that could assist you."

"I appreciate the honesty. Even if it's not great news and I may still be some weird anomaly, it's more info than I've gotten in over thirty years."

"We're all clear and have a deal?" She extended her hand.

I grabbed hold, noting how firm and sure her handshake was. We shook on it, deal struck, all ready to proceed.

I started for the door after we'd agreed to meet at her house for training the next day.

Harley called me back, a hint of a smile on her face. "By the way. Haven't had a chance to ask yet. The tall woman you hang with at the café, the one who looks sweet, a bit like you in the face. She your sister or something?"

"She's not your concern," I called back. I didn't stop my exit, hoping to shut her down with little fanfare. I knew I shouldn't. Merry was curious. Now Harley seemed curious. Couldn't stop myself, because the idea of my sister in any way involved in this mess was too much for me at the moment.

IT HAD BEEN A long day, but like some masochist, I made it longer with a little heavy reading. After a dinner alone and time spent mindlessly watching part of one of my comfort movies, *Interview with the Vampire*, I cracked open the book on the Starry Wisdom Cult.

It was chock-full of fun facts about the group who had tried to capture me for whatever reason. They apparently started up in New England in the nineteenth century. Some professor founded the cult after a trip to Egypt, where he'd discovered something about an Outer God named Nyarlathotep, also known as the Crawling Chaos or the Prince of the Dreamlands. Some all-powerful dude who could flit between the Dreamland, home of the Outer Gods, and Earth. Which was odd, because if he already could come to Earth, why were these cultists all hell-bent on bringing him here? Seems he'd come and go as he pleased if he was a god of some kind, but what did I know of the logic of Outer Gods and cults?

Regardless, Starry Wisdom was no good, like Gareth and Harley had said, at least from the account given in the book. Its members tried to use ancient objects to call up something called the Haunter of the Dark to give them secrets about the world and beyond. The author linked them to a bunch of disappearances over the years, and more than a few people had been hospitalized for mental trauma after encountering the cult. They disappeared many times from different places over the years, but they always came back somewhere else, and always came with some big black church structure. It was a secretive group with no known leader, though the petite blonde was in the running, in my mind.

It was interesting—or at least would be if this wasn't a real group of people who had really tried to kidnap me. As for those real people in this place and time, the book told me nothing new. All I knew was they were out in a weirdly rural spot in the middle of Upper Arlington, a non-rural, fancy section of the Columbus metro area. There was a creepy church blacker than the night sky and it gave off seriously questionable vibes and sounds. A tiny woman with a heavy twang and a pretty-girl look seemed to call at least some of the shots. They wanted to do something with me out on the shelter grounds. Oh, and they liked cookies and cupcakes, possibly.

I needed more. More about the cult, more about Gareth and Harley. If my old shadow world was now a part of my real-life world, I needed to know more about myself and what place I had in all this mess. Everyone wanted something from me. I got that much, but I didn't get what exactly it was I had to give, and why they'd all worked so hard to get it.

SEVEN

HARLEY LIVED IN A sleek condo in the Short North. At one time, the Short North had been cooler, hipper. With the campus expansion and the general push toward gentrification everywhere in the city, it had become posher and more polished. There used to be kitschy bars and restaurants, even a few dives here and there. It had been more fun then, in my opinion. Now it was all tall buildings with fancy bars and restaurants and shiny new condos like Harley's. Nothing against Harley for having it. It showed she was successful at whatever she did.

"What do you do for a living?" I couldn't help but ask. Sometimes my mouth shot off before I could think better of it. "Sorry if the question's rude or whatever. Just wondering, seeing as I know you fight evil at night. Is this a Batman situation?"

"I'm no billionaire playboy," she said with a chuckle. "Though my parents are long dead."

I paused and put my hand on her forearm to stop her before she could move down her hallway. I wanted her to look me in the eye when I said, "I'm sorry to hear it." Because I was. It caused my heart to ache. I hurt sometimes simply missing my parents. They'd moved to Florida, into semi-retirement, a few years ago. It was hard not having them as close as they always had been. Thinking of them forever gone to me was rough.

Harley didn't joke or blow off my sentiment. She gave a solemn nod before saying, "Thank you. They were good people who died in a car accident many, many years ago. A hard loss, most definitely, but it was a blessing of sorts."

I cocked my head but didn't push. She swallowed, looking at me as if trying to make some decision. "It was the early eighties. At the time, I was already deep into the occult, a fully-fledged mage. My parents weren't a part of the occult world. Never had been. They knew nothing about it, and I was dreading explaining it to them. If they'd lived to old age, I would have had to. Because of these."

She turned her arms out, exposing her wrists and inner forearms. Barely visible on her dark skin was a mess of intersecting circles with no real pattern I could decipher. They marched a straight line from wrist to inner elbow. Unlike her other sigils, these had a slightly different tint to their color, almost like the purplish glow of a black light.

"These are extra special. Took a lot of effort, a great deal of magic from me and the man who put them on me, to get them to stick to my skin. This halted my aging, an unexpected side effect, but it is what it is."

"Why do it? Ink something on your body that can have unintended consequences?"

"Seemed like a good idea at the time," she muttered, finally turning away, and I took it as my cue to drop the conversation. For some reason, the topic was veering too close to something she didn't want to discuss with me, even if she had shared moments before. She had every right to withhold pieces of herself. I wasn't going to pry.

Harley slipped her hands into her crisp beige slacks and spun on her shiny loafers to saunter down her hallway. I followed without being told to, taking in what I could as I went, but it wasn't much. The hallway walls were painted a soft taupe and had nothing on them. I didn't get to see more of her living area because she turned into a doorway, which led down a flight of stairs. Those opened up into a stark-white, cavernous room that appeared to be part library and office space and part CrossFit gym. An odd choice, but whatever.

"Sure you're not Batman? This seems a little Bat-cave-like. Plus, a two-story condo? In this building? Sheesh."

"I've lived a long time. Made a few lucky invest-ments. I also sell and procure occult books and arti-facts, which can be lucrative if you're good at it." She grinned. "I'm very good at it. I take on mage tutoring occasionally, which is how I know Gareth."

"You're a magic teacher?"

"Don't get it twisted, Randy. I'm not someone called to teach and willing to give over all of myself to some random student. I tutor when and if I wish, depending on many factors, but at the end of the day, it's still a job, not my life."

"Does this mean you expect me to pay you for your time?"

"No. We have a unique arrangement, though it's no less transactional. It's more barter-based than cash-based. I help you, you help me."

"Are you going to tell me, beyond a general good-of-humanity line, why you're so hell-bent on taking down Starry Wisdom?"

Her eyes darkened for a moment, and she clipped out, "Yes." Nothing else came, so I figured it was a tale for another time, like her forearm sigils, and dropped it.

I moved to the library area because I saw a faint glow washing over everything. Shimmers, in a wide variety of colors, dominated the space. It was full of sigils. On books, on cases, on the floor, on the walls. They were all over the room. The library space had a mass of them all cramped together. It was almost hard to look at it head-on, with the never-ending glow bouncing around the white walls.

She must have noticed me squint or something because she said, "The white reflects and adds an extra oomph." Moving deeper in, she picked up a large black leather-bound book and flipped through it a moment before off-handedly tossing it my way. I fumbled to catch it as she said, "You'll need to start there. It's a fairly remedial text on sigils."

Harley sat at the large office chair rolled under a computer desk. Her laptop popped to life, but she ignored it, turning the chair around to face me. She gestured for me to sit in the large armchair across from her. It was nice of her to give me the comfy seat.

As I wiggled onto the fluffy, oversized chair she obviously used for reading, given the piles of books all around it, she began. "I have to admit, I'm slightly unsure where to start with you. I had a friend overnight me the book in your hands because I didn't have anything for beginners in my collection. If and when I instruct mages, I serve as an advanced tutor of sorts. You need something with more introductory information. However, you're not exactly a novice, seeing as you can naturally perform magic most mages can't even execute successfully."

"You did it," I said, referencing our short times together in the shadow world.

"I'm not most mages," she answered, as if it was a simple fact. No brag or boast, only truth.

"Given everything, we're going to start with a more scattered approach. As far as study goes, we'll begin with info on magic, the occult on our plane, sigils, and so on. The knowledge part is where you need basics. The practical part, how to control what you already have, may need more advanced training." She pointed at the CrossFit section of the room, and I marked its even more aggressive glow, as well as some suspicious-looking dark spots along the floor and wall. "If you're going to protect yourself and help me, you need both, but you need to do them simultaneously. Don't think Starry Wisdom will wait around too long before knocking on your door again."

I swallowed hard, running my hands over the cover of the book as I stared at a large mark on the far wall. It looked suspiciously like a massive scorch mark.

"This will be taxing. Mentally and physically. Are you ready?" she asked.

"No," I said honestly, "but it doesn't seem like I have much of a choice."

"You don't. Not really," she said. "Though you could choose to ignore all of this, go on about your life suppressing your power and pretending there's not a cult out there after you. Not the smartest choice, but you could choose it."

"I thought I could, for a minute."

"You came around eventually, which is good enough. It tells me you want to do this, and maybe we can get some shit done together."

I nodded, not nearly as certain as Harley but bolstered by her words anyway

"FOCUS," HARLEY SAID CURTLY, as she stared at me from a few paces ahead. We'd moved from the library to the magical workout area because she thought for our first lesson we should combine practical application and information in one go. She told me to stand in the center of the room, raise my hand to shoulder height, and look for the shadow there.

"On what?" I asked. "You snapping 'focus' at me doesn't really tell me what to do."

"You know what it looks like, yes? The shadows clinging to you?"

"I've seen it in the other world. I see it every time I'm there. The other day, I saw it out of the corner of my eye. First time I've ever seen it here."

"Let me think a minute." She paced back and forth, and I fidgeted until she walked up to me.

"Explain to me exactly what it is you see when you are in the shadow plane."

I told her about it all. The shadows were darker. They grew and morphed, almost like they breathed in the black-and-white reflection of the everyday world. I even described the sounds of monsters in the distance. I didn't tell her I'd seen one once. I couldn't describe the horror of it, and even in this bright room in the middle of the day, I was afraid to speak about it.

When I finished, I shivered at the memories, but she either disregarded it or didn't notice. "Very good. Your perception of the shadow plane is exactly as it should be. Your natural magic shows you the same view as a mage. It's an important thing to note, so we know we aren't working from different perspectives. We'll back it up then."

She moved closer, leaning in as if to chat about everyday things. "Magic is simply energy certain people have learned to harness, like how Tesla harnessed electricity with alternating currents. Way back when, some person felt magic somehow and used it. Others followed suit. Those who can feel it can draw it forward from our surroundings. It's in the air. It's in objects. It's in nature. It's everywhere, so if you know how to pull it from a source, you can focus it in another direction. Mages operate by collecting these natural magical elements out in the world. They pull magic from one place and put it to use in another way." She squinted at me and continued. "You, though. You don't need to pull magic. Magic somehow pours out of you. At least some magic. Enough to attract shadows."

"But shadows are just shadows, the results of light and objects in space together. They're not sentient."

"These are," Harley said, as she passed a hand slowly through the air about an inch above my arm. "They may not be as intelligent as humans, or more like they simply don't possess the same type of intelligence we do, but they know. They act. They also flock to you, for whatever reason. These here aren't regular shadows. They're what most mages refer to as the Deep Dark—shadow and darkness which can move and think and do so with some encouragement."

"You're saying this Deep Dark, a collection of some-how-sentient beings, crawls all over me?" I asked, my voice rising in pitch at the implication. It was hard to breathe. The idea of it was so creepy.

"Yes. Which is why you want to focus and gain some control. They seem to like you, but it'd probably be better if they weren't always hovering all around your body. You want them to answer your call, not cling to you without purpose."

"Like Lassie, but with thinking shadows and dark-ness."

Harley laughed. I frowned. It was my joke, but still. None of this was funny.

"Randy, you see it in the shadow plane because mag-ical energy and things composed mostly of magical energy, like the Deep Dark, are more visible there. You can see them here too, if you focus."

"Again, what do I focus on? Because looking at my hand isn't doing a whole lot."

Harley stepped back a few paces once again and said, "Let's do some guided meditation. Close your eyes."

I did, seeing darkness and, for the first time, won-dering if anything hid there in the dark behind my eyes too. "Now, think about the last time you were on the shadow plane. Fix the memory in your mind, concentrating on what your hand looked like there."

I followed her instructions, remembering and focus-ing for long minutes with my eyes closed.

"Open your eyes, look at your hand, and remember."

I did. And I remembered. I remembered the last time, when Harley dragged me into and out of the shadows, plus all the other times in my life I was there. All the times those shadows seemed to slip and slide along my skin like a soft caress, like a phantom hug. I remembered how I used to play with them when I was a child, moving my hand about in waves of darkness and giggling at the shapes they made for my amusement. At one time, we had connected. I remembered the connection, and I finally saw, ever so faintly, a wisp of a shadow clinging to the back of my hand.

"There it is," I whispered, awed. I turned my hand over, and it moved, shifting to my palm.

As I looked at it, it became darker and it grew, until I could see it crawling up my entire arm and down the rest of my body.

"I see it. I see it!" I was excited, slightly giddy from childhood memories of playing with the Deep Dark, but as soon as I thought of it as a thinking, living thing, the panic came on. "I see it everywhere. It's everywhere, Harley. How do I stop it!"

"Calm down. You're okay, Randy. I promise. You've had this swirling around you since at least the first time I saw you. From what you say, likely since you were a baby. If it was going to hurt you, it would have done so already."

I knew, logically, she was right. Still, my skin crawled, and not with the Deep Dark. Goose bumps prickled my skin, and my stomach rolled. My head pounded.

"I don't like this at all."

"We're going to try something. They come to you naturally, so maybe if you focus on a purpose, they'll move away. Intention is key to all magic. Watch my hands." She made a sign in the air, tracing a star in a circle—a pentagram—with her finger. "A very basic sigil, a personal sign of protection you've likely seen before. Big with everyone, even those who dabble but don't fully get magic. It also is a sign of personal space and safety. I want you to do the same as I did. Draw the sigil in the air. As you do, think about wanting space, wanting peace, wanting control over yourself and your body. Got it?"

I nodded. Did as she said. Nothing.

"Again," she called.

I did it again, over and over, for ten minutes, until the Deep Dark shivered around me and, like a puff of smoke, evaporated. It didn't leave, however. It manifested as a small pitch-black ball which hovered near the corner of my eye. Creepy, yes, but not nearly as creepy as having it all over my skin.

"Nice," Harley said with a smile. "No offense, but I thought you'd take much longer." Clapping her hands together, she said, "Now, on to more complicated things."

I groaned. I felt drained, mentally, emotionally, and physically, but we carried on, the small ball of Deep

Dark hovering at the corner of my eyesight all the while.

Eight

THE NEXT FEW DAYS were busy. Trying to make time to bake for the cafe, stay on top of up my catering-and-special-order business, and hire new staff would be enough for anybody. Add new magical training and dusty-old-book study sessions in the mix, and it became too much. I was burning the candle at both ends, although with me getting more used to the Deep Dark—which I'd started calling DD for short—if my candle did snuff out, I might be okay in the darkness.

Harley knew a little about DD, and she and Gareth both did a deep dive into sources in various languages I couldn't read, to help me along. She thought getting me more comfortable with the shadows surrounding me, and eventually me learning to use them, was the best course of action. My magic-leaking body already manifested or attracted it, so why not add to it, I guess.

It was a crash course for everyone, in a way. I was learning basic sigils, the bare minimum for things like protection and defense, mostly. As Harley learned more about the shadow magic, we experimented with offensive sigils to direct DD. It worked well. My protective sigils needed more force, more oomph. Any sigil I used to focus and command DD worked like, well, a charm. The more I learned, the more at ease I felt with the golf-ball-sized DD hovering in my peripheral vision all the time, and the more connected we became. It felt oddly like a pet I was training to do tricks. I could sense resistance in my mind when it didn't want to do something, for whatever reasons. I felt a flair of happiness when it accomplished some task. It seemed to want to please me, which might have been creepy if I stopped to think too long about it, but as it was, having some shadow entity on my side seemed like a good thing, so I wasn't going to question it too much.

I could get DD to expand, contract, and zip about a room. I could give it weight and mass, so it became a projectile or a cage, whatever was needed. It was a handy little thing, especially as it was always near and always ready. I needed to memorize a few sigils and focus my thoughts, and it could perform these basic functions well enough to give me more peace of mind.

The cult hadn't returned for me in the dead of night or anything. I hadn't even seen anyone around, unless they cloaked their magic when out and about in public. One of my growing powers was being able to spot magic and sigils more easily. Harley and Gareth both helped. Harley's sigils glowed stronger the more I focused on seeing them. She was like a beacon, brighter when she had more magic and softer when her sigils of holding were low. Gareth actually became darker. His tattoos turned blacker and deeper, emitting a muted, almost hazy light at the very edges. Apparently, this was because he hadn't gone through a special sigil process, he'd simply mixed sigils into normal tattoos. I didn't want to know what the special process was. It had to be pretty bad if Gareth wouldn't do it and Harley didn't want to go into detail about it. Luckily for me, I guess, I didn't need it.

See, sigils both called and focused magic. To have them permanently written on the skin made it easier for mages to call forth the magic and focus their intention. Because I didn't need to call forth magic, for whatever odd reason I was different from every other human out there, the simple tracing of sigils would do. Harley could even do some basic magic if she reserved enough in the weird battery-like sigils on her body, by envisioning the sigil in her mind. She figured with more practice and knowledge, I could get there too.

I was a week into training, and I had already learned a bunch. However, I'd always been my harshest critic, which was why I was now muttering expletives to myself in my kitchen while Gareth and Harley watched in silence. It was the first time they were both present, as I usually talked with them separately. Harley had told me she wanted another training session, and I had told her it had to happen in my kitchen. I had a load of baking to catch up on, and surely magic wouldn't disturb cupcakes in my industrial oven, right?

She and Gareth showed up and, for the last forty minutes, had been trying to help me get a complex sigil-intention combo down. This one was supposed to allow DD to surround me, like it used to always do, and then project outward, a bubble with physical force. It was a bit of defensive and offensive magic combined, hence the more complex sigil. Gareth had found it in one of his books and brought it to our training.

I stared at the page, traced the complex slashes and swirls with my finger, before taking a deep breath and trying again. It was super tricky, because DD had to become more manifested when in contact with me, then push outward. The part about it surrounding me and becoming solid was working well. It was the projecting outward in a bubble part I wasn't able to do.

I sighed and shook my head after yet another failed attempt. "I can't get this."

"Sure you can," Gareth said gently. "You're doing great."

"You're not concentrating hard enough," Harley said. "You need to maintain focus. You get through the first part and think you've got it and your focus shifts. Or you get distracted by the shadows on your body, the unfamiliar weight of it. Whatever it is, there's a mental hiccup." She checked the book again, a small crease between her thick, dark eyebrows as she studied the sign. "You've definitely got this down. You're drawing it well, but that's the simple part. You need to push your mind more."

At the declaration of my failures of mind, my buzzer sounded. I moved to grab my oven gloves and remove the cupcakes before they over-baked.

"Doesn't help, you're trying to multi-task," she said as I slid out the pans and moved them to a cooling rack.

"I need to pay bills, so you'll have to deal."

"I'm not the one being hounded by an evil cult."

"Here's the thing. I haven't seen anything to do with the cult since that night," I said, after slamming down my mitts and turning back to her. "I've seen a lot of you two, but no more from the cult."

"What, exactly, are you implying?" Harley asked a little too slowly.

"Now, ladies," Gareth began, but both Harley and I raised our hands in the air toward him, simultaneously shushing whatever peacemaking attempt he was about to throw out.

"No, Gareth. Let her speak her mind."

"Yeah. I will. I've been working my ass off, learning all this new stuff, and it seems like there might not even be a point to it. Danger isn't exactly lurking around every corner right now, if you know what I mean."

"They nearly killed you," Gareth said softly.

"I know! I'm not an idiot," I yelled. "I also know they could pop up at any moment. I'm just saying, maybe all of this is happening too fast." A little softer, because I hated to admit it out loud, I said, "Maybe it's all a little too much for me to handle."

Harley snorted. "Nice pity party."

"Excuse me?" I hissed, annoyance and exhaustion and self-consciousness warring inside to make a very volatile mixture.

"You heard me." She stepped forward, head cocked to the side, staring at the dark spot at the side of my vision, at DD. "You think this is a sign of weakness? It took me decades to get to my mage level. To become the best of the best. And here you are, stumbling around and performing spells I could barely do after years of rigorous training. Get a damn grip."

"Is this supposed to make me feel bad? I didn't ask for this!"

"No one asks for any of this type of shit in life!" Harley yelled, getting closer. "You think I asked for the crap I have to deal with because of who I am, what I look like, who I want in my bed? No. But it's there, and I have to deal. Dealing with that shit over decades is tiring, let me tell you." Stepping back, she scoffed. "You've had a week of this."

"I've had a lifetime, if you remember."

"Oh, excuse me. A lifetime of running from it and a week of doing something about it after someone almost sacrificed you to an Outer God."

"Okay, okay, okay," Gareth called, physically stepping between us. "I think we all might need a break."

"Agreed," I said between clenched teeth.

Harley said nothing. She turned on her heels and walked out the back door without a word. Tears pricked my eyes. There was anger and resentment there, but also guilt, embarrassment, and a little self-pity, like Harley had said. I walked over to a stool and plopped down.

"You shouldn't be too hard on yourself," Gareth said. After some hesitation, he said, "Or Harley."

I deflated. "You're right. I know you are. It's hard, and it's been a long while since I've done something hard. Baking came easily. I was good at it early on, so I kept at it. I also enjoyed it. This, though, takes a lot of effort and, because of all the crap connected with it, isn't nearly as much fun."

"Understandable. People gravitate toward what they know and like. It'll take time and energy for you to get into magic," he said, moving to lean on the workbench beside me.

"How did you even get into all this? Harley told me a bit of her life, but not about how or why she became a mage. How does it even happen for someone who's not like me?"

"Harley's story is hers to tell, but there are two general ways into this life. One, a person has something horrible happen to them because of magic or the occult and gets obsessed. Two, a person stumbles upon something when reading or studying or exploring and becomes obsessed."

"Are you one or two?" I asked softly.

"One," he answered, sadness clear in his eyes.

"You don't have to tell me," I replied, but he stopped me with a shake of his head. He looked away before beginning his story.

"You know I'm not from here originally, right? I'm from Oregon, actually. Did a lot of hiking and camping as a kid. In my late teens, my friends and I used to go out often, deep into the wilderness. It's beautiful but deadly out there. We always thought danger would come in the form of a bear or mountain lion. Should've been more cautious, but we were young. Invincible in our minds, if we even considered mortality at all back then. One night, a man popped up in the darkness around our tent. We shared our fire with him when he asked to warm himself. He had no pack, but he clung to an old leather book as he sat silently in our circle. We were making noises to go to bed, to get him to move along, when things changed."

Gareth paused a moment, like he needed to gather himself to continue. "I didn't know what was happening, but he started chanting what sounded to me like gibberish. We were on the coast, and he compelled us down a cliff. I don't know what reason he had. Sacrifice, appeasement, sheer evil. Didn't matter. We tumbled over the cliff one by one into the sea, against our will but through the compulsion of our own bodies. I was the last to go over, so I watched it all happen as I screamed in my head to try to get my body to listen, to do something. It didn't."

His eyes were misty, distant, and I reached for him, a pang in my heart for what he had experienced. "They called me lucky. I hit rocks instead of waves and landed at a weird angle. The pain of the fall broke whatever spell was cast over me. Also broke my leg so I couldn't get myself out. I lay on that rock for hours before some fishermen spotted me from the water. I told people what happened, and it got me a stay in a different type of hospital. When I got out, I stopped talking about it and started studying. Got into dark corners of the internet. Studied old books in archives in college so I could learn even more. I found out magical affinity had allowed my mind to stay intact while under the man's spell. I took my growing knowledge and my affinity and worked on honing my skills, becoming a mage, always thinking, in the back of my mind, I'd run into the guy again someday. I haven't found him yet, but it's a small world, this occult business."

"What happens if you find him?"

"I like to think I'm gentle by nature, but if I run into him…"

I nodded. He didn't need to answer. The horror of it, the shadow in his eyes when he talked about it, was enough for me to guess and not judge.

"Thank you for telling me."

"We all have our own burdens and agendas in this world," he answered. "You have something you need to do. So does Harley, and so do I. We mesh, but we can't forget it's different things, unique experiences, driving all of us. Making us who we are."

"How'd you get so smart?" I asked, half joking to lighten the mood.

"I'm not that smart," he whispered, bringing his hand up to cup my face. "If I was, well, I'd be thinking a lot more about all those personal reasons I have to continue and not obsessing over the way you nibble your bottom lip when you're concentrating on something."

I gaped, a flash of heat paralyzing my body. For a moment, I thought he was going to kiss me. I wanted him to kiss me. Whatever held him back snapped into place, and he stepped away from me.

"Give Harley a call later. She's not one for extended apologies or grudges over arguments. Say you're sorry, she'll say the same, and it'll be like it never happened."

"Thanks for the talk."

"Any time, Randy." With a small parting wave, he followed out the same back door, into the night, into the shadows.

NINE

GARETH HAD BEEN RIGHT. Harley wasn't one for extended apologies. I'd learned early on she did not text back, so I called her.

Harley answered the phone by saying, "What?"

"I'm sorry for being an ass last night."

She sighed. "Happens to the best of us. Come over tomorrow for training."

The call ended.

We picked up where we left off, in a way. Harley felt I needed more time to learn proper focus before I tried complex magic again. I sat in her magic CrossFit room, meditating and focusing while she threw things at me—or yelled or sat in silence—before jumping up to run at me. My task was to stay focused no matter what she did. It was difficult because Harley was inventive and, honestly, intimidating at the best of times. I got better after several sessions. I could concentrate, block out outside distractions while still processing what they were and reacting if need be.

We didn't practice the complex sigil I'd tripped over before, but I kept it at the back of my mind, a personal goal of sorts.

MERRY AND MIA PUSHED their way to the counter, where I was restocking after a mad Saturday lunch rush.

"Hey, stranger," Mia called. It wasn't nice and singsong-y. It was accusatory but, granted, also warranted. I'd kept up with our text thread, the exchange of quips and memes and random chitchat we'd had. I hadn't called or hung out in about two weeks, which was at least ten days too long. I'd side-stepped their direct questions again, but it appeared it wasn't going to fly any longer.

Merry smiled sweetly, choosing to let Mia take the lead so she didn't have to get her hands dirty. She didn't fool me. She had as much of a hand in this as our little sister, so she got the same side-eye as Mia.

"What do you two want? I love you both, but I'm kinda busy here."

"Please. You have two employees behind you and a case full of tasty treats."

"Because I filled it seconds ago, genius," I shot back, holding up the now-empty trays in my hand.

"What you're saying is you were busy, but now you are no longer busy."

"Ugh. Again. What do you two want?"

Merry finally waded into the conversation. "We're going to see a movie. Come with us."

"I have baking to get done." I wanted to go, but I was being more hesitant with my sisters, pulling back because of the chaos surrounding me. For their own good, of course, though they didn't know it, the horrible busybodies.

Mia looked around, assessing the entire café with her intelligent eyes. "Your lunch rush is over. You have enough to hold until you close. Do you have a special order for tonight?"

"Not exactly..."

"Then you don't need to bake anything right at this moment. You can come to a matinee and bake later if you have to, but not before we have a movie-and-dinner lady date."

I opened my mouth to decline but didn't get anything out.

Merry leaned in, her eyes a little tight and glossy, something that made my stomach flip with guilt. "Please, Randy. Please come hang with us today. Even if only for a few hours."

I looked between both sisters, one poised as if she wouldn't take no for an answer, the other looking like she might cry. I sagged in defeat. I was going to a movie.

It was no real hardship though. One of my favorite places in Columbus was the Gateway Film Center, which was where Merry and Mia were headed. I insisted on driving myself separately, so I had an escape route. I was hoping a quiet movie theater would halt conversation and I could slip away before they wrangled me into dinner, as Mia had suggested.

We settled into our seats, ready to watch the latest foreign horror movie on offer, which meant the theater wasn't too crowded. In fact, it looked like our group of three, along with two couples, were all who would show up for the afternoon showing.

Merry munched popcorn on my left while I leaned to my right and whispered my opinion of the previews to Mia, who responded with her own critiques. We weren't savages; we never talked during the actual film if we could help it, but previews were fair game.

As Mia was talking about the pros and cons of some new indie drama coming soon, my eyes shifted away from the screen and landed on a faintly glowing sigil shining like a beacon in the dark movie theater. It was on some dude's hand, and when the dude next to him shifted to climb up the side stairs, I saw a similar glow.

My stomach tightened, and the black beside my eye drew heavier in response. DD was giving me a warning of sorts, but I was too stubborn to listen. I figured I'd wait. Maybe they were mages or dabblers, nothing nefarious.

I should've known better. When they scanned the rows of seats, they both stared when they found me, and I knew I'd made a mistake. Luckily for us, we were on the opposite side, near the first staircase closest to the theater exit. When the pair moved into our row, making their way right toward me and my sisters, I jumped up and hissed, "We have to go. Now."

"What the hell?" Mia yelled. Merry coughed, like she'd swallowed a piece of popcorn weird because of my outburst.

I pointed at the men quickly advancing on us in a menacing way my sisters finally noticed even if they couldn't see their glowing sigils. "Follow me. NOW!"

I scrambled over Merry, who jumped up after me, dragging a sputtering Mia behind her. We hit the doors. I bolted for the hall and grabbed Merry's hand to keep them close as I headed for the escalators. We ran down and out the bottom doors into the cluster of shops around the theater in time to see the men running down the stairs behind us.

"What the hell, Randy?" Mia yelled again as I kept running.

"No time now. Get to your car and go. They'll follow me, not you."

"No," Merry said, digging her heels to the concrete as we rounded the entrance to the parking garage. Our cars were side-by-side on the first floor, a perk of an early afternoon showing. It also gave us a perfect view of a man with the faint glow of sigils on his pale hands leaned against my car. Right in the way of our escape. Right in the way of my sisters.

DD shivered at the corner of my eye, ready to work. Mia was asking questions. Merry was rigid and straight, stoic even. I focused, as Harley had taught me. The men chasing us slowed behind us, knowing we were trapped between their little triad of cultists.

The man at my car, a tall lanky figure in an ill-fitting black suit, gave a smile that didn't reach his hard eyes. "Miranda Carter. A pleasure." He gave a slight bow. "There's someone who would like to speak with you."

"I'm sure there is, but I've been busy, so they'll have to take a rain check."

"No. We insist." He looked at me, trying to shield my sisters. "Or, if you like, we can have a different conversation with Meredith and Mia Carter."

I didn't see red. I saw black. The threat made rage claw up my throat, a dark beast ready to do damage to any and everything standing between my sisters and safety. My focus crystallized due to all the training from Harley. DD quaked on the outskirts of my vision, ready and willing to do my bidding.

They had trapped us, and I knew in a matter of moments, one of the three cultists would touch a sigil or start a chant to snag me, and likely my sisters, in some magical snare I would have no way to escape. I hadn't learned about magical escape plans yet. I had one option floating in the back of my mind, and somehow, deep within me, I knew it would work then, even though it had not worked before.

I sketched the complex sigil I'd learned days before, funneling all my intent, all my rage, into creating a safe space for my sisters. I flung my arms around Merry and Mia, making them crouch with me as DD reacted to my call. It all happened at once. DD took on mass, which made it visible, right before it cloaked me and my sisters in a hardening, protective shell of shadow. Then it ballooned outward, creating an enormous bubble with us smack dab in the middle. It gave the men no chance to retreat, and luckily there were no random bystanders in its path either. It pushed out far enough to fling the three men in different directions, each slamming hard into concrete or block walls or, in the case of the one who had been by my car, a small Prius. The protective bubble tapped a few car bumpers too, pushing the vehicles into the surrounding walls or other cars, which resulted in the sudden and deafening blast of several car alarms blaring at once.

"What the hell?" Mia asked once again. Shock was making her a little repetitive.

"Did you do this?" Merry whispered, looking wide-eyed at the filmy black bubble of Deep Dark surrounding us.

"Yep. No time to explain now." I stood to crane my neck around, making sure all the cultists were down. I didn't think they were dead, only knocked out cold, but I didn't have the time or inclination to check. I pulled my sisters up from their stunned crouch and clasped a confused-looking Mia on the shoulders. "Are you okay to drive?"

She looked around, shock still on her face for a moment before my question, and the implications, registered. Her face hardened, the infamous Mia resolve and grit snapping into place as she nodded.

"Good. Get in the car and go. Now. Before these guys wake up."

"Are you going to do anything else to them?" Merry asked, hesitant to leave.

"No. I'm running."

"We're coming with you," Mia declared, unlocking her car as we all headed for our thankfully unscathed vehicles.

"No, you're not. Go home. Stay there and don't come looking for me. In fact, don't come see me at all until I tell you it's safe."

Merry gave a harsh laugh that sounded so out of place coming from her, it made my heart ache. "Not going to happen. Mia, follow her wherever she goes. I don't care where. We stay on her."

I didn't have time to argue, what with the likelihood of the cultists waking up any second and the certainty someone else would come running because of all the car alarms. "Ugh. Fine. Get to Warm Regards ASAP. There's at least some protection there."

As I scurried for my Mini Cooper and cranked her to life, I sent a mental thank-you vibe to DD, which was once again hovering in a little ball at my peripheral vision. I peeled out of the garage, turning right to take Fourth Street to avoid N High Street traffic. We needed the wards Gareth had put on my place to help protect us from whoever or whatever might try to follow. As I flew down the busy street as best I could, weaving through the lanes while also keeping Mia's car in my rearview mirror, I told Siri to call Harley. The wards were good and all, but we needed all hands on deck if these bastards were coming after me, and my sisters, in public places now.

Ten

Like weeks before, and because of the same damn people, I screeched into the small lot behind Warm Regards. I was out of the Cooper and unlocking the back door when Mia's red coupe slipped into the one empty spot left. With the door held open by my foot, I waved my scurrying sisters into the building. I wasn't 100 percent sure where the protection spells Gareth had placed on the building began, so getting inside as quickly as possible seemed like the best bet.

I'd barely slammed the door shut and locked it before Mia and Merry were on top of me, demanding answers.

"What just happened?" Mia asked as she paced back and forth in front of my large workstation, her arms waving about in angry gestures as she spoke. "Those guys came out of nowhere. You somehow knew they were after us. And they were. They totally were. They chased us. And the creepy dude in the suit sitting on your car? So weird and menacing. Not good. Not good at all. And the black bubble thing! What even was that?"

Merry didn't have to say anything to add her own weight to the irate questions. She pulled her brows together in a deep furrow. Her stare was silent but sharp. She rubbed her upper arms as she crossed them over her chest, a silent gesture of fear that gutted me as much as Mia's pacing and rapid-fire questions.

"Okay. Okay. Look, I didn't want to get you two involved in all this mess. It's too dangerous. I'll tell you what's going on, but you have to promise not to get involved. In fact, it might even be best for you two to pack up and go visit Mom and Dad for a while, get out of Columbus."

"Are you fucking kidding me?" Mia screamed, stopping her pacing to turn on me. "No way are we leaving you to whatever this is circling around."

"You don't understand..."

"Then tell us," Merry said, finally interjecting. "Tell us what's going on and let us decide what we should do next."

"Uh-uh, not going to happen. You two went ballistic during the divorce. I cannot have you doing the same over this. It's way too dangerous."

"We're not stupid!" Mia yelled at me, her angry voice trembling with hurt or worry or a combination of both. "What we watched you do back there was beyond. It was something I've never seen."

"It was something to do with your powers," Merry said.

Mia nodded. She was right, neither was stupid. There were no stupid Carter women. They'd likely ferreted it out together on the ride over here, then presented a united front against whatever bullshit I was likely to throw at them. And I wanted to throw bullshit. Make up something to explain away what had happened, to assure them I was safe, to make it all seem not a big deal, but nothing was coming to mind.

As they stared at me, expectation and impatience lined with worry and love marking every taut line of their bodies, my resolve crumpled. Partly because I had no time to make up something plausible, and partly because these were my sisters, my best friends, my rocks. It'd feel damn good to have them as emotional support for all the shit stirring around me right now. On top of everything else, they might well be targets. The cultists knew who they were, knew their names. Information was power, and not telling them, not letting them know what's out there, could leave them vulnerable in the future.

I shook my head, blew out a harsh, audible breath, and began. I gave them a condensed version of events, but I gave them everything: the weird black church, the attempted kidnapping, Harley and Gareth, my new magical training, and a little about what Starry Wisdom was. I'd come to today's events and the spell I had performed with DD, which I mostly glossed over, when a loud banging at the back door had all three of us jumping.

I creeped toward the door cautiously until I heard Harley's muffled voice yell, "Let us in, Randy. We're exposed out here."

I threw open the door to find Harley, in her regular attire of leather shoes, dress pants, and buttoned-up shirt. Gareth, however, stood dressed for the gym, with sweat making the tank cling to his very defined and displayed muscles. It was enough to make me stare a moment, even with all the fear and anger rushing around in my veins.

He blushed—straight up blushed—and ducked his head before muttering, "Sorry. I was working out."

I stopped my ogling and got back to business. "No worries. Come in. Please."

Mia gaped at Gareth, likely as stunned by his big, tattooed form as I had been a moment before. Merry shivered and smiled back at the sly grin Harley threw her way. I sighed, knowing after this there likely was no stopping whatever might happen between those two, and I had no place to stop it anyway.

"Harley, Gareth, this is Meredith and Mia Carter. Merry and Mia, this is Harley Warren and Gareth Davis."

Gareth gave an open, encouraging smile and reached forward to give each of my sisters a firm handshake. "A pleasure, ladies, although I wish it were under differ-ent circumstances."

Harley gave an acknowledging nod, though she let her stare linger on Merry for several beats before she straightened and got down to business. "You said Starry Wisdom cornered you in a parking garage?"

"Yeah. At Gateway. Two of them found us in the theater first and chased us out to the garage, where a third was waiting."

"How'd you get away?" Gareth asked, his tone harsher and more clipped than I'd ever heard before. He obviously was not happy about the situation.

"Well, about that. Seems in my anger I can pull off complex spells I failed at before."

"Really," Harley drawled. "Not a big surprise, as heightened emotions and a need to defend can make people do extraordinary things in a time of crisis. Add in your magical ability and connection to Deep Dark, and you get a potent mix."

"More like a giant, protective dark bubble with some bite," Mia groused.

"What did you see?" Harley asked, staring at Merry for a response.

"It was all kind of a blur, really. Those guys had us trapped. They were talking about taking Randy somewhere to talk to someone, maybe taking us as well, and then suddenly, it was like a dark haze popped up around us. It pushed out, knocking the dudes from their feet, even knocking into some cars. I could see through it, but it was like it made the world a few shades darker."

"Good. Good. You've now done it once, Randy. Means you can do it again if need be."

"Hopefully, the need won't be," I countered, but I stopped being flippant and looked right into Harley's eyes. I wanted her to know I was being deadly serious. "They wanted to take me. They threatened my sisters to make me comply. I knew they'd do it too. Take me and them for some horrible end. You weren't there, but you were, in a way. What you taught me about focus and stuff, it sank in and kicked into gear when I needed it most. When my sisters needed me most. I can't… I don't know how to thank you for that."

Harley nodded, but it wasn't a dismissal. She met my gaze, hers hard and dark, and I knew she understood my thanks were genuine. I was now firmly in her corner because her corner had helped me protect my sisters.

Gareth, who'd been quietly observing, stepped toward me, crowding my space to take my hand in his. "Are you okay?"

"Yes and no," I answered honestly. He squeezed my hand in response but did not let it go. Instead, he twined our fingers together and stood at my side, holding my hand. His much larger one was warm and reassuring, so I didn't protest.

"We talked about this before," Harley said. "The possibility the cult would try to come after you again. I doubt it will stop any time soon. It might even ramp up after the power they witnessed today."

"Fabulous," Mia said in a sarcastic, shrill tone. "What, exactly, are you going to do about it?" she asked, looking between Harley and Gareth.

"We—Gareth, Randy, and I—are going to take down the cult," Harley answered back.

"There are no other options?" Merry asked, still clearly worried.

Harley's eyes softened, as did her voice, when she said, "I'm afraid so. This cult, they pop up every few decades, cause havoc wherever they are, and then they disappear. They'll keep coming for Randy unless we stop them. They will not stop on their own. I was already on them, trying to work a plan to take them down. Gareth was helping because he agreed to help me. Randy is now a part of it too. If she wants to stay safe, to keep you safe, she doesn't have much of a choice."

"She mentioned us going to Florida. Why can't we all go? Get out of Columbus and stay out until whatever they're doing blows over?" Merry asked, looking for other ways to get out. I understood the impulse to get far away.

"At this point, with her demonstration of power, I think they'd follow her wherever she went," Harley answered.

"I can't," I whispered. "This cult, they hurt people. Kill people. I couldn't live with myself if I ran and let them do harm to others here in Columbus."

Gareth squeezed my hand again in support and understanding, though he made no additional comment.

"Ugh. Heroes, the lot of you," Mia said with a scoff, as if it were a bad thing. "Fine. We stay and we fight."

"Oh no, no, no. I can't run, but you can."

"I can't leave you," Merry said, straightening and planting her feet firmly in a defiant stance. "I won't. If you're in this, we're in this."

Mia jumped in. "Merry and I can't help you physically or magically or whatever, but there are probably other ways we can help. I can snoop around online."

Harley looked Mia up and down. "A basic Google search won't be very helpful," she said.

Merry, Mia, and I all laughed, and Harley cocked her head in response.

"Trust me," I said. "Mia goes far beyond Google."

"White hat?" Harley asked, which was surprising. She knew enough to ask, which not many her age would. Made me think, with her work, she'd probably been in some dark corners of the internet.

"Far more gray than white," she replied with a grin.

"Excellent," Harley answered. "I know enough, but someone with real experience could get us into interesting places."

"Wait a minute," I called, stepping up, though I couldn't go far because Gareth didn't let go of my hand.

"Mia's good. She can handle it," Merry said. "I can't offer much but grunt work or financial analysis, if you run into any type of accounting and need to understand it. If so, I'm your girl."

Harley smiled her way, her voice on the edge of a purr, when she said, "We'll find something for you to help with, hon."

"I said wait..." I huffed, but Merry stopped me.

"No, Randy. We know what's going on now, and you can't expect us to turn a blind eye. Like you said, we can't sit by while these people do nasty shit to our sister or to anyone else in our city. We're not going to go out and fight these cult people, but we can help, and you should accept our help."

Mia and Merry both stood facing me, their arms crossed and hips jutted, the perfect image of Carter sister defiance and stubbornness. I didn't have it in me to argue.

"I need you to stay away from this as much as you can, at least physically. If you promise you won't go out and do stuff to make you clear targets, or clearer targets than you already are, I'm fine with you helping. Occasionally." After thinking a second, I quickly said, "If you agree to let Gareth ward your places and your cars and your workplace, Merry." I looked at Gareth, a soft smile on his face. "Is that cool? Can you create wards for them, like you did here?"

"Of course. I'd be happy to. I'll even do one better." He pulled three slim leather bracelets from his pocket, each stamped with various sigils. "Personal protection charms I made a few days ago. I'd planned to give them to you soon anyway, for you and your sisters."

I reached for them, happy to have something to give to my sisters, but he halted my hand.

"For this, you need to do something for me."

"What?" I asked, hesitating slightly.

"Train with me."

"I already train with you and Harley."

"Yes. You do all your magical training with Harley with occasional assistance from me. I want you to physically train with me. Magic is great, but there might come a day when you need to fight, and I want to be certain you know how to protect yourself in all the ways you can." Real concern shone in his eyes, and it tugged at my heart. Also tugged at other parts of me, but I pushed both aside for the moment.

"Sure. We need a schedule because I still have to work, but I guess can add kickass fight training to the rotation."

Eleven

Gareth told me to meet him at the same gym where I'd cornered Harley, so I strolled in there the next afternoon. I'd spent the morning doing much-needed but always-dreaded administrative paperwork in between baking ruby chocolate éclairs—and the never-ending batches of cookies, muffins, and standard cupcakes I always stocked. I knew I'd soon need to hire an assistant for the kitchen, someone who could take over some of the more routine bakes so I could focus on the fancy things and the special orders, but baking was my happy place, and I wasn't quite ready to let someone into my place yet. Though, with the rate of training and magical research and practice and the occasional attempted kidnapping, I'd likely be putting out feelers sooner rather than later.

Shoving my sunglasses up, I looked out to the sea of stares once again. Only this time, Gareth was giving me a friendly wave from behind the fighting ring. When I reached him, I saw he was on a mat like they used in wrestling. The Greco-Roman kind, not the WWE kind. He wore similar clothes from the day before, a sleeveless shirt and long shorts, his muscled physique on full display. I took him in from head to toe and didn't hide the fact, which made the mountain of a man blush a bit and fidget. I gave a quick snort at the fact I made this muscled mage nervous.

"Thanks for meeting me here," Gareth said, waving me into the circle pattern on the mat.

I laughed. "I should thank you, big guy. You're the one teaching me to protect myself."

He shrugged and moved on. "From what I remember, you did a few things the night you met Starry Wisdom that looked like learned defense maneuvers. Did you take a self-defense class at some point?"

"Yeah. Me, Merry, and Mia took one. It wasn't too in-depth though. Two two-hour sessions total."

"It's still a great place to start, Randy. Means you know some basics and practiced on a mat before. All good things for me to know."

He had me tell him what I knew, walk through some of the maneuvers on my own. It came back slowly but surely. Still, after ten minutes, I'd exhausted my knowledge of self-defense. When I admitted as much, Gareth waved off my concerns.

"You're doing great. You got out of the situation with the cultists, so what you knew helped you. Did what it's supposed to do. It served you well."

"It helped because I also used my magic to nope out of there real quick."

He moved closer, coming within inches of me. His calming aura once again took effect, making me feel all warm and gooey in a way I wasn't used to experiencing. It also seemed stronger, and I didn't know if it was because of his usual pull on me or my growing attraction. Regardless, my heartbeat kicked up a notch, and my skin tingled at his closeness. DD even shook slightly at the edge of my vision, as if it responded to his proximity as well.

Gareth, his voice low so it wouldn't be overheard, said, "It's a good thing, Randy. Anything you have at your disposal, use. Magic, physical objects, or defense training. Your first objective, always, should be to stay safe, and it's perfectly acceptable for you to use whatever it takes to keep yourself safe."

I nodded, knowing he was right, and he stared a beat, his chest showing his deep inhales and exhales before he closed his eyes, righted himself, and took a large step back. He turned to gesture at a dummy sitting on a black pedestal behind him. The thing looked like a man, at least a man's head and torso. It didn't have arms. Reminded me of those CPR dummies except ready to take a beating. "Let's see what you can do with this guy."

For thirty minutes, I punched, slapped, kicked, and kneed. Gareth had me repeat moves over and over, and he corrected me every time my form was off. He was nice about it, gently instructing me about the best way to throw a punch to the gut or throat for maximum effect. It was definitely an odd juxtaposition, the gentle way he taught me to hurt a person, but I appreciated it. I liked Harley's blunt, no-nonsense approach for sure, but Gareth's gentle guiding hand felt right in the moment.

Or maybe it was because Gareth felt right. The feeling he gave me intensified throughout our training until it was a practical weight in the background, blanketing my body. I was sweaty and tingly and achy in the best of ways when he told me our session was over for the day.

"Next time we'll work on direct attacks, if you're okay with us working hand-to-hand," Gareth said as I took a big gulp from a cool bottle of water he'd handed me.

Wiping my sweat and eyeing this gorgeous man who made me feel both safe and buzzing, I smiled widely. "We can work hand-to-hand anytime, Gareth." I winked, he blushed, and I chuckled.

I thought nothing more would happen, we'd keep the dance up for a while still, but he stopped me after I picked up my keys and sunglasses from the bench along the wall.

"Randy, um, I was wondering. Would you like to go on a date with me?"

I did a double take. I didn't think he'd be the one to ask. I hadn't asked because there was too much shit swirling, but I also wasn't going to turn him down. Whatever this feeling was between us, I wanted to explore it. First, I needed to ask one question.

"You need to tell me something first. Have you used magic on me?"

"What? No. Never. What do you mean?"

"I don't know. I feel something when we're close. Wanted to make sure you weren't causing it."

Gareth grinned, then asked, "You feel something? What exactly?"

"None of your business, big guy. It's my feeling," I answered with a sly smile.

It was his turn to chuckle, a deep quiet thing that sent a shiver across my skin.

"Still good to know, but again, no. I haven't bespelled you to make you feel any type of sensation around me or say yes if I asked you out."

"Good. Because I want to go out with you, but not if you used some sigil to make me compliant or something."

Gareth turned serious and said, "Those things exist, and there are plenty of people who could or would do such a thing. It's one reason it's good to keep your bracelet on at all times." He gestured down at the leather band he had given me the night before, which I'd totally forgotten was even there. It already felt like it belonged on my arm.

I stared at it myself and swallowed hard. Regular people used force and coercion enough; I didn't want to think about bringing magic into the mix. "Right."

"Hey," he called, stepping closer to put a finger under my chin to lift my face toward his. We stood, me staring up at him, him staring down at me, for a few beats. "We're going to make sure you and your sisters stay safe. Okay?"

"Okay," I whispered.

"Now, when do you want to go out? What do you want to do?"

I thought for a moment and realized what Saturday would bring. "You ever been to Heatwave?" I asked. Heatwave was a dance party. It happened once a month at a bar in Old North, close to Warm Regards. The DJs spun vinyl records and played mostly sixties and early seventies R&B, Soul, Motown, stuff like that. It was always a good time, and I did love to dance when I had the chance.

"No, but I'd go with you."

"Do you even know what it is?" I asked, still close, still breathing him in, still staring right into his soft and kind hazel eyes.

"No, but I'd still go with you, no matter what it is."

It was my turn to blush a little. I stepped away, feeling all flustered and nervous and needing a little space from him.

"Meet me at my place Saturday night around nine."

He smiled. I smiled back, then gave a jaunty wave and slipped my sunglasses back on as I strutted out of the gym. I put a little extra pep in my step so he'd have a nice show as I walked away.

THE NEXT DAY, I walked out of the kitchen into the café around the lunch rush to restock pastries. To my surprise, I found Harley chatting with one of my employees, Yasmiin, as she made Harley some frothy drink with the machine. When I got closer, I could tell they were speaking a different language. I thought it was Arabic, but mostly because I knew Yasmiin spoke English, Somali, and Arabic, and it didn't sound like the first two. When Harley noticed me, she gave a small salute. Yasmiin looked over her shoulder to see me. "Oh hey, Randy. Want me to put those away when I get done with this?"

"Nope. I got it. You keep on the coffee machine and we're all good," I answered with a grin. Turning slightly to Harley, I asked, "What brings you here? Aren't we supposed to meet at your place later?"

"Yes, but I need to reschedule. A business thing came up."

"Not a problem, but you could've called or texted."

She held up a coffee and a pastry. "I come here, I get treats. I text you, no treats."

I laughed and waved her around the counter to follow me back to the kitchen. As we moved, I said, "You can also get free treats. A perk of knowing the owner."

"You can't always give things away for free. Not the best business decision."

"I don't always, but for you, the person now training me in all things shadowy and magical, I think I can spare the occasional coffee and cheese danish."

Harley cracked a smile for once in her life and said, "Noted."

We both leaned back against the counter, side-by-side, heads turned to look at each other. "Anything else you needed besides rescheduling and coffee?"

"I also need you and Gareth to do a little recon for me tomorrow, if you can. I have to drive out of state for the night for this business thing, and we're losing time with Starry Wisdom. We need more direct info if we can get it. Maybe you and Gareth go in the daylight, search the surrounding area, find out things from neighbors if you can."

"I'm no spy master, but I'll do what I can. Are you thinking daylight is better?"

"Starry Wisdom relies on secrets and darkness. They hide. Daylight activity is likely not something they do often."

"They tried to kidnap me, possibly Merry and Mia too, in the middle of the day."

"True, but I think it was desperation brought on by Gareth's protective wards. They're strengthening for some reason." She eyed me a moment and bluntly asked, "Are you and Gareth fucking?"

"Not your business, Harley," I said. I wasn't offended by the question. It just wasn't her business. Plus, I hoped maybe we would be soon, so I didn't want to say anything about it.

"Fair enough." She took a big bite of her danish and a pull of her coffee, holding both up and looking at me, a silent compliment of sorts.

"Danish was all me, and I do them well. Yasmiin is the coffee master. It's always stellar when she works the beans here. Speaking of, were you speaking with her in Arabic?"

"Yes."

"Didn't know you knew Arabic. Do you know Somali too?"

"No."

"How'd you know she spoke Arabic?"

"Took a stab at it because of the hijab."

I nodded. Made sense. It also made me wonder more about Harley, who she was, why she did what she did.

"How many languages do you know?"

"A lot. I studied linguistics at Stanford."

"In the sixties, right? Lots of stuff going down in history then. What was it like?"

"Racist while trying not to be. Like a lot of things, then and now. People don't like to admit as much as stuff's changed, it's also stayed the same."

I couldn't comment on it, because I wasn't alive back then and because I was white, so I nodded to her. It was a weak confirmation or acknowledgement of her experience, I knew, but a confirmation in the moment at least. She continued eating, and I let her finish her danish in peace before I peppered her with more questions.

"Why do you do this, Harley?"

She looked at me for a minute before she answered. "There isn't one singular reason. Nothing traumatic happened to me. I stumbled into the occult a long time ago and was drawn to it. Something in me connected to words and language all my life, and because of it, I also connected to sigils and magic when I discovered them in dusty old books. I had an affinity for it, though no inherent power like you."

"What about Starry Wisdom?"

Harley's eyes turned hard. "In the early nineties, they popped up for a year in a different Midwestern city. And people went missing—the type of people most don't care about when they go missing: sex workers, immigrants, drug addicts. I noticed, and I also noticed magic about in the area. Traced it back to them, though they left before I could stop them from moving on. In and out, taking lives with them for whatever reason.

That's their MO. I've wanted to shut them down ever since."

"You're like some vigilante?"

"No, but I do think we need justice and fairness in this world. If we don't find it for ourselves, or help others find it for themselves, no one else is likely to do it."

Sad but all too true, so I stopped questioning her. I told her I was good with recon if Gareth was good with it, and she gave me a wave as she strolled to the back door, one hand in her trouser pocket as she flung it open with her other one and walked out into the bright spring afternoon.

Twelve

THE NEXT DAY, MIDAFTERNOON, I'd made a boatload of cookies and cupcakes and had started work on a wedding cupcake order. I didn't do wedding cakes, didn't need the hassle and pressure, but I'd do dessert tables and cupcake displays for weddings sometimes. This one was fairly simple, a mixed assortment of some of my standards in a large, tiered platform with flowers and such. Easy peasy, as far as wedding things were concerned. I baked all the cupcakes first, would ice and decorate later, and do basic set up on Saturday morning, the day of the wedding. Saturday was also the day of my date with the big guy currently leaned against a motorcycle in my back parking lot.

"Not gonna lie. When I first saw you, this is what I imagined," I called, gesturing toward his tall frame effortlessly lounged against a large bike. I was no expert on motorcycles, but this one was pretty. Not big with chrome, but big, black, and still somehow sleek.

He pulled his sunglasses down and gave me a look that would turn most women into goo. Though I'd like to think I'm made of sterner stuff, it made my knees a little wobbly and my breath hitch a touch. "When I first saw you, I knew you'd be everything you've turned out to be," he said.

I stopped in my tracks. It was likely the best compliment a man had ever given me, so I deflected and turned a sly smile his way. "You charmer, you," I replied with a joking tone, wanting to defuse the swell of feeling his remark caused. "What's the plan? All Harley said was she wanted us to do a little recon, but I'm not really the spy type, so I don't exactly know how this works."

Gareth handed me a helmet as he said, "Nothing strenuous or too dangerous. We go around the site, not *in* the site, and see what we find. Snoop, if you will. If we encounter anyone in the neighborhood, we ask a few simple questions, see what comes up. Our main objective is to see if we can discover how much activity has been going on at the site and for how long."

I paused then, something suddenly coming to me. Something so obvious I couldn't believe I'd never questioned it before. "Why were you there weeks ago, when they tried to take me? Were you following me?" Gareth and Harley, before I knew who they were, had been in my café that day. There'd been a moment with Merry and Harley, one my sister had talked about all afternoon, so I distinctly remember them being there. Then they also popped up later in the night when I discovered all this stuff and was nearly being tied up and tortured or whatever. One million new things had popped up since then, so I hadn't thought about it until now.

"No. Of course not," Gareth said, and he seemed genuine. "We had done similar recon, figured they had something planned because of the information we gleaned, and wanted to stop them if we could. Or help anyone who might need it."

"Did me being there mean you couldn't stop them outright?"

"There were more Starry Wisdom cultists than we expected. We did not think their numbers were above a dozen. Obviously, we were wrong. As good as Harley and I may be, we could not have battled fifty members wielding their own magics."

"You stepped in to help me."

"We stepped in to help you escape. It was all we could do in the moment. After we saw you disappear, and Harley realized what you'd done."

"Okay, so we know they want me, likely because of my abilities or whatever. What else do they want here? I mean, they didn't show up in Columbus because of me, right?"

"We don't fully know. They performed some big magic about a week before they tried to take you. We don't know what it was, but there were traces of it all over the place afterward when we did our recon. It was powerful and may well be why they needed you. Large reserves of magic take a long time to replace."

"I was going to be their magical backup battery?"

He nodded solemnly, and I swallowed. They had already done something big and were planning something else big and needed me to help amp up their magic stores to keep doing whatever evil crap they had planned. Not good at all. As Gareth had told me, if I lost my magic, I'd likely lose my life. I liked my life where it was. Didn't want it sucked away.

"Gotcha. Our mission today is to make sure they aren't ramping up for something else big yet."

"Exactly. We both can see and sense magic, so we can tell if a large group performed a big spell recently. Standard investigative practices, like interviewing potential witnesses, also help put pieces into place."

"Cool, cool, cool. Let's get at it then," I said, gesturing for him to get on his motorcycle before I slipped the helmet over my head. He did the same, waiting for me to climb on behind him. As I did, his calmness enveloped me. A zap of lust also kicked in as the engine revved. I circled my arms around him, scooting up to mold my thighs around him, pressing my core against his backside. His aura or whatever, his smell, his feel, all combined with the tremor of the machine beneath me... It was a good time for sure, and I laughed at the heady joy of the mesh of feelings as Gareth pulled out of the back lot with a rev of his engine.

RECON WAS KIND OF a bust. We learned a few things Gareth said were significant. There was a soft glow of dissipated magic in the air. It was like neon had leaked into water, something bright fizzling out and bleeding into nothingness. Disconcerting, especially when Gareth told me it was the same big magic they'd seen weeks before fading. Of course, I couldn't see it the night I'd come this way, because I wasn't open to seeing magic yet, but knowing it was even more pronounced weeks ago made me nervous. Gareth hadn't been exaggerating about the levels then. Something big and likely dark, given the cult's usual MO, had happened in this area.

We steered clear of the site, but not clear enough a tiny peak of the black church wasn't visible. I saw its steeple above the tree line, and that was enough for me. It shimmered in my sight now, but not brightly. It was like night and stars made into wood and roofing slate. The shape stood out against the light-blue sky almost like a void, an absence, as if someone had cut out the steeple in reality and what I actually saw was absence. Very weird.

The weirdest thing, though, was the feeling. The dissipating magic was a hard drum, like a headache threatening to rear its head after lack of sleep. Whenever I had the steeple in sight, I felt a rush of heat in my blood and a weird compulsion to move closer, to see, to touch. A vibration also sounded in my body, as if a string connected my guts to the black church and something in there was plucking on it, trying to send some message down the line. None of it was good, and it somehow felt too personal to share with Gareth. May be a bad call, but I wasn't telling him what the black church did to me or how it made me feel.

We didn't see anyone when we were out and about, so no old-school PI questioning happened. All in all, it was an enlightening but frustrating spy mission. Gareth dropped me back off at Warm Regards with a promise to see me in a few days for our date. I got a different tingle, one of clear anticipation, and sent him on his way with a sexy smile and a jaunty wave.

But of course I couldn't have an afternoon to decompress after being all in my lusty and magical feels. I walked into my apartment and found Mia watching some YouTube gamer stream on her laptop as she sat eating a cookie at my kitchen bar.

"Yes, please, help yourself." I said with sarcasm dripping from my voice.

"I will, thanks," she replied. Mia and Merry had all the keys, and I'd found them in my place many times before, so it wasn't a shocking surprise. A little inconvenient, but not shocking.

"Saw the hottie drop you off on his motorcycle. Nice. Would have thought he was a Harley dude, but a Ducati fits too."

"How do you even know these things?"

"I know a little about a lot," she said, and I rolled my eyes in reply. But she wasn't wrong.

"What do you want, brat?" I pulled up behind her and gave her a big hug, my snark at odds with my actions.

"Ew, get off. You smell like exhaust and magic biker dude," she said as she patted my hands affectionately. That was how Mia and I were. We bantered and teased, and we both enjoyed it.

I pulled back and rounded the counter to lean across from her. "What gives? Is this a simple sisterly visit or..."

She turned her laptop to situate it between us, clicked out of YouTube, and pulled up a document. "I've been doing some research."

"Maybe not the smartest thing to do, Mia," I said, my fear for her a twisting knife in my gut. She didn't need to be on anyone's radar more than she already was.

She waved a hand as if shooing away my big-sister concerns and continued. "Harley and I chatted about what she might need from me, how I could help her, and, by extension, help you. I'm not the trusting type, so while I've been working on this stuff, I also dug into her and Gareth."

"What'd you find?" I asked, my curiosity getting the best of me.

"They checked out, which was super boring. Harley gave you her real name, like her original name, which was surprising. Her legal name, or what she uses to function in society now, is different, but she was born Harley Warren. Same with Gareth Davis, though he doesn't have any aliases. He's connected to some weird accident out in Oregon years ago, but I figured magic, you know?"

"Yeah, he told me."

She nodded and continued. "All that is good. They seem to be honest about who they are and what they do."

I arched an eyebrow at her in question. "What exactly is not so good?"

She answered after blowing out a deep breath. "I've done lots of research over the years into your abilities. Nothing. It's mainly because I didn't know where to look. Research is all about knowing where to look. Once Harley gave me some direction, specifically about the occult and areas where certain people into magic could discuss things like Starry Wisdom, I was off and running, exploring very deep corners of the internet, ones I hadn't even seen or known of before, which was surprising because you know I'm no stranger to deep, sometimes-dark things online. A lot of what I found about Starry Wisdom and the Outer God they seem to serve brings me right back to you."

"What do you mean?"

"This god thing they worship? He's called a lot of things and known for a lot of things. None of them wholly good or bad, more ambivalent, as you might imagine a god dude to be if such a thing existed, which, apparently, it does. Or at least Starry Wisdom thinks it does."

I nodded but circled my hand, urging her to get to the point.

"Okay. It seems this Outer God, the only one who can come and go from Earth as he pleases, has an affinity for shadows. As in, he can manipulate them, control them, call on them, and use them whenever he wishes. Especially the thing called the Deep Dark."

I stood up straight and still. DD, as always, hovered in my periphery. Mia went on. "Randy, from what I found, no person has ever had this before. A few old human gods in ancient pantheons, sure, but no humans. And this Prince of Dreamlands guy is one creature in this jumbled Outer Gods magic mess who can consort with shadows or whatever."

"That means..."

She finished for me. "What you can do is somehow related specifically to the Outer God these creepy cultists worship."

I slumped down on the counter, putting my forehead to the cool stone. I always worried, always, about what I was, what it meant—even before all this mess with cults and gods. If what I did related back to this worshipped Outer God specifically, then was I connected to the god too? Was this why the cult was after me? And did it mean I was evil, like the cult?

"Hey, Randy?" Mia called gently.

I twisted my head to the side so I could look at her with one eye, because she'd pester me until I did.

"This is all new info, and not fully researched. I'll dig deeper. I just... I wanted you to get this from me first before I went to Harley with it."

"Appreciate it," I said halfheartedly.

"Randy," Mia called, firmer, her grit and fire on full display in her eyes. "Again. We do not know what this means, not fully. Not yet, but I promise, we will."

She reached for my awkwardly flung out hand and squeezed it tight. "We got this. I swear. We'll find out. The bright side is we are finally finding out things, more than we ever did before, about your powers. We'll get to the bottom of it. Promise."

I nodded, swallowing hard, worry and wild scenarios stampeding through my brain. Mia saw it, responded with a soft grunt of her own, and came around the counter to me, draping herself over my body. It was nice, the weight of her against me, the tangible feeling I knew was love. It helped, in the moment. What would help more would be a chat with someone more equipped, someone more knowledgeable about all this.

Mia loved me and wanted me to know things, but to not worry. It was a losing battle. Mostly because I hadn't given Mia all the info. Couldn't now, because it felt so much more sinister after she'd told me what she knew. I didn't voice what I had experienced during recon, what I felt around the black church. It was almost a kinship, like somehow I belonged in the area, my body or magic or whatever drawn to whatever was hiding there. None of that boded well for me and my magic, its source, and what it might mean about who or what I was in all this.

What it meant was I needed to talk with Harley. Pronto.

Thirteen

I called Harley to tell her I'd be by her place a little later, to discuss what Mia had found more in-depth, so she knew the direction of our conversation.

I was bone tired, not going to lie. I'd been baking, running my business, training in magic and defense, reading basic magic and sigil primers, and worrying all the time. It was a lot. Too much, maybe. The next thing on my to-do list was to hire a solid baking assistant to at least take some of this load off. Being a small business owner didn't exactly mesh well with trying to learn about my magical abilities and save the greater Columbus area from an evil cult. Made me think about superhero films in a whole different light, mainly in terms of logistics and hours of sleep.

Harley was nonchalant, as per usual, when she let me into her condo. We headed for the office to chat. It looked like she'd been in full-on research mode. She'd scattered texts all around, her laptop was open to some online text, and sigil diagrams littered the floor. She'd obviously been looking into what Mia had uncovered.

"I take it this is why you wanted to chat?" she asked, sweeping her arm across the room.

"How'd you guess?" I said deadpan, flopping down on the mostly empty armchair. Mostly empty because one stack of books rested on its arm instead of the enormous pyramid lying on the desk seat. Harley didn't sit, instead falling into what I thought of now as her signature cool lean against her cluttered desk.

"Mia came to you first." It wasn't a question or an accusation, simply a statement of fact from Harley.

"Yep. Really wouldn't have expected anything else if I'd thought about it more. Maybe something you want to think about when you give her assignments."

"I'm not in the business of withholding info. I don't care if she tells you first, as long as she gives me everything later."

"Good to know," I said, then let silence fall for a solid thirty seconds. Harley gave me the space to get at what I wanted to ask.

"Some of the stuff Mia told me, it didn't sound great."

"Like what?"

"Like the connection I seem to have to the Outer God the cult worships, but there's more. Stuff Mia doesn't know. Stuff no one knows." With a deep breath, I let it out. Told Harley all about the weird feelings I'd had at the black church.

She thought for a moment before she said, "Honestly, we don't know enough to think about it as good or bad, Randy," Harley told me. Honest to a fault, maybe, but honest nonetheless, something I always appreciated but desperately needed right now. "The info on Crawling Chaos isn't exactly new, though Mia uncovered some interesting accounts even I had never read. With everything she discovered about the god and the cult, her reasoning, connecting you and your powers more firmly to the Prince of the Dreamlands, appears to be accurate." All was factual, and also worrying.

I chewed my lip nervously as more silence stretched between us. Harley eventually said, "Spit it out, Randy. What are you worried about?"

"Does this mean my power is inherently bad? Or I'm inherently bad?" It was something lurking in the back of my mind all my life. It was hard not to think it, when I was so different, and darkness and shadow marked my difference. The cult wanting me, wanting to use my power for their definitely-not-good purposes, also made it seem like whatever was in me might be actually not good.

Harley started to speak, then stopped herself for a beat before she continued. "I'm going to give you a few answers. The first you won't like, which is I don't know. I truly don't know the source of your powers or the reason you have them. It is unfamiliar territory for me. I know magic. I know bits and pieces of what you can do, but why you can do it and what it might mean further down the line, I can't rightly say."

She moved then, stepping to the chair and crouching down to look me in my eye. "Still, you have to realize this concept of good and evil you cling to is all relative. It's contextual, even for ordinary humans. What one person views as good or bad can change. That's the way it's always been for people. Some may argue there are universal goods and evils—charity and murder, for example—and I would agree. In the end, it all boils down to what you do in this world with what you have."

I blinked and let out a shuddering breath as Harley continued.

"From all I've seen of you, I'd say you're good. If you're good, you can use your abilities to do good. The action is what's important."

"Even if I'm connected to some evil god out in the cosmos somehow?"

"Nyarlathotep isn't evil, per se. He is a being out of time and space, existing beyond our realm of under-standing, so human concepts of good and evil can't fully apply. If we tried to apply them, it would be more accurate to say he is ambivalent, as many humans are. A powerful creature capable of both good and bad."

"Mia said something similar. Even if I have powers similar to an Outer God, it doesn't mean I'm bad, be-cause Outer Gods aren't all bad."

She straightened, sliding her hands down her slate-gray slacks to readjust them after her lean, and popped her hand back into one pocket. "All non-hu-man magical beings, Outer God or monster or some-thing else, are dangerous. They have vast stores of magic they can use, but also they can be so very human and inhuman at once, connecting actions and motivations with amazing abilities. Doesn't make all of them bad or all of them good. Doesn't even make any one of them bad or good throughout all of time or space."

"Still wouldn't want to come upon one in a dark alley somewhere."

Deadly serious, Harley flatly said, "You best hope you don't come across one anywhere."

HARLEY'S COMMENTS, THOUGH NOT definitive answers, were helpful. As long as I was in control of my power, and my power didn't control me, I could do good. The lingering worry whispering in the back of my mind late at night was that one day, my power would take over and I'd lose my control. But, as my mom liked to say, I shouldn't borrow worry. There were too many unknowns swirling around in everything, including my magics, so I needed to focus on what I knew and what I could do.

This included having Merry review my books to make sure I was good to hire at least one baking assistant to help ease my workload. She gave me the thumbs-up, so I spent a good chunk of the evening writing and posting a job ad online. Afterward, I put another plan into action.

There was a small storage area next to my apartment. It was a long, narrow concrete room where I put extra supplies and whatnot, though I had great organization downstairs, so it stayed mostly empty. Now, it was going to become my practice room.

Harley knew a lot about magic and the occult, but she also, by her own admission, didn't know a great deal about my magical abilities in particular. She could help me in theory, but practice was becoming iffier. It seemed time I stretched my wings on my own.

Which was a scary idea. I'd spent most my life ignoring or actively stifling my abilities. Hell, my ex-husband hadn't even known about them, and we had been together for years. Now I was using them, more and more people knew about them, and they still felt new and unknown. Maybe more than anything, I needed to spend a little alone time becoming acquainted with whatever it was inside me.

With solo testing firmly in mind, I took out the dozen dusty supply boxes from the closet, stuffed them in various locations downstairs, and surveyed the empty space. The door was sturdy, the walls were concrete block with no windows, and the floor was smooth concrete. It honestly looked like a basement, even though it was on the second floor. A safe place to be alone with my magic. If it worked out, I'd ask Harley or Gareth to give me a little extra protection with some wards. Or maybe ask them to teach me how to ward a place myself.

There was a naked lightbulb in the center of the room, so I dragged my mostly unused yoga mat into the space and plopped down under it. The position of the light meant there were long shadows clinging to each wall, which I imagined was good for my magic, since it seemed to like shadows so much. Or at least attract shadows.

Can't say I was an expert or anything. I had no clue what I was doing. I simply sat there with myself for a few minutes, thinking, before I used some of Harley's focus exercises to make my mind turn inward, try to find my magic and poke at it a little, see what happened. After meditating for a long time, I opened my eyes. Nothing. Total bust.

I regrouped, shaking out my arms and twisting my neck and shoulders, and went back to center. This time, I started with visualization. I put myself in a comfortable place: my baking kitchen. It gleamed in my mind, all stark white and shiny stainless steel. My imagination put me inside my body, standing at my cleaned steel worktable. I stared there, letting any stray thought float away before it clung to me, simply looking down at the prep table and the hazy quasi-reflection of myself I could see in the surface.

The reflection eventually became more solid, more real, as if I wasn't looking at a table but a mirror. It was me: dark-brown hair pulled back in a slightly messy bun, old black T-shirt and dark-purple leggings, my smirk, my nose, and the shape and position of my eyes. But those eyes weren't mine. Instead of a deep navy, they were all black. Not even any whites around the iris, but full-on black. Black as a shadow. Black as death. Then my mouth in the reflection opened wide, and black smoke as thick as ink curled out, wrapping up and out into the air between me and the table. I tried to step away, but I was stuck. I even tried to blink out, pull my mind back to reality, where I knew I sat on a yoga mat a floor above the prep table, but stayed right where I was.

I was stuck as the slow rolling smoke billowed, grew into a deep cloud, and washed over me like a wave. It didn't feel like smoke; it felt like water. Water from the darkest, most unknown depths of the ocean filling my mouth, my eyes, my ears. I tried to block it out, but it seeped in, leaking into my being. When I opened my mouth to scream, it rushed in, choking me, filling my stomach and lungs in seconds and cutting off all my air.

All I had, all around me, was rolling, inky waves. It was me and darkness, and darkness was winning. I shuddered, then struggled, then bucked my body, but there was no escaping the void filling me to the brim, encasing me inside and out. When I thought I would die swallowed up into nothing, a sound like the soft strum of a string quaked through me. Something inside my body pulled me up tight, and suddenly I was no longer afraid. I no longer struggled but let go, and in that moment, the rolling darkness dissipated and fell into me softly. It didn't engulf me but become one with me. The inner string vibrated again, tuning itself, righting me. When my eyes cleared, I once again saw my clear reflection in my pristine worktable, black eyes and all. I watched it smile as I felt my mouth do the same.

I came to, no idea how long after, with my body sprawled across the yoga mat and my face pressed to the cool concrete floor. The light shuddered and blinked, as if coming back on. My body was slick with sweat, and my ears popped and cracked as if readjusting to a new pressure. A new depth.

Pulling myself up on slightly shaky legs, I made my way to my bathroom, horrified at what I might see in the mirror when I looked into my eyes. They were normal and navy blue, dark but not black. No signs of inky darkness were anywhere except where I'd gotten used to it, with DD hovering right outside my vision. There was a soft tingle in my hands, the feeling of coming to from sleep after having lain in an awkward position for too long, but otherwise I was fine. I was good. I felt strong.

There was a new thrum in my mind. It felt much like the plucked string from my vision. A controlled darkness, taut and waiting within.

Fourteen

Other than the thrum now living in my gut somehow, I didn't physically feel weird or different, but what had happened during my improvised guided meditation nonsense still freaked me out. I had to chat with Harley about the experience. She asked me a million questions and called me a fool for attempting such a thing alone, without consulting her or having more knowledge or research. I countered with the fact it seemed like I was some type of anomaly in the magic world, so no amount of research could get me knowledge more helpful than trying things on my own, which resulted in a lot of huffs and sighs from her, but no outright claim I was wrong. She finally demanded I create an anchor, whatever that meant, but I told her she'd have to tell me more about it later. I had no time Saturday. I needed to finish the wedding cupcakes, make the delivery, and get ready. It was time for my date with Gareth.

THE WEDDING CUPCAKE DELIVERY didn't result in any kidnappings or discovery of new magical people, which was a plus. Meant I had plenty of time to get all fancy for my date.

My outfit was on point. The bar where Heatwave took place could get hot—stifling even, with all those bodies moving together to the music. I dressed accordingly: red pleated skirt that hit me mid-thigh, black V-neck shirt, which molded nicely to the curves of my boobs and belly, chunky heeled ankle boots, and my leather jacket. I chose the boots because I wanted a little height but wasn't about to break my neck dancing in anything too spiky. The jacket was for aesthetic mostly, though Ohio spring nights could turn chilly quickly. I added some sparkle with a layer of shiny silver necklaces and a ginormous pair of silver hoops. I even went glam with my face and hair, big smoky eyes and pouty maroon lips under a sleek but full high pony, which was also good for heat and dancing. It was all dark sexy, which was my general vibe, but slightly understated. A solid first-date outfit for going out with a man who'd never seen me in anything other than work or workout attire.

No surprise, Gareth rang the bell on my downstairs apartment entrance right on time. To the second. I'd heard his bike pull into my lot a good seven minutes before then, meaning he'd waited patiently to ring on time rather than early. I'd been ready for a while, the heady anticipation of a date enough to spur me on. Plus I was more often early than late. Hated being late. It made me anxious, which meant I was bounding down the stairs as soon as I heard the first ring sound.

I saw Gareth standing there, hands in his jean pockets and a small smile on his face. He'd cleaned up his beard, trimmed it to be a little closer to his face, a little less wild. I liked the other look, his wilder blond beard a touch on the Viking side, but this was good too. Showed his handsome face more, while also telling me he cared about our date. The second part was the most affecting, to be honest.

He wore slightly baggy dark-wash jeans and a white button-up shirt. He'd rolled his sleeves up to his elbows, putting his lovely, tattooed forearms on full display. A thrill snaked up my spine as I looked at them, thinking about them wrapped around me as we danced. As we did other, more carnal things. Heat hit my face, but I pushed it aside to give him a wide smile.

"Hey there," I said brightly.

"Hey," he said, his voice more gravelly than usual. His eyes also roamed, something they rarely did before. He seemed to like what he saw, as he closed his eyes for a beat and took an audible breath before sending a sexy smile my way.

I'd never seen that smile. He'd grinned, smiled openly, and sent me kind and encouraging smiles over the weeks I'd known him. This smile was heat and promise, a little wickedness tamed to some extent. It made my heart flutter and my core clench.

It was his turn to chuckle darkly, knowingly, at what I must have telegraphed on my face. He reached a hand forward, snagged one of mine, and brought it to his lips, placing a soft kiss on the back of my hand as if we were in some Regency ballroom or something. "You look…" He didn't finish his thought.

Always ready to play, I quipped, "Hot? Sexy? Your every fantasy come to life?"

He speared me with a heated gaze. "As tasty as any of your cupcakes."

Another woman might not respond to a line about cupcakes, but I turned gooey inside at the compliment. It showed he knew me and appreciated more than the outward trappings, though he did obviously appreciate all on offer. I smiled, big and open, then dipped my chin and batted my lashes in a flirty acknowledgment before saying, "Back at you, big guy."

Gareth laughed and pulled me close, as if he couldn't help it any longer, couldn't keep from touching my body. He didn't lean in for a kiss, only held me in his arms, looking down at me with a sexy smile firmly in place. "You ready to go?" he asked softly.

"Yep. You ready to dance?"

He nodded and let me go so I could lock my door and lead the way. We walked the few blocks down North High toward the bar, our hands clasped and smiles on our faces. The calm always hovering around Gareth encompassed me, though it felt a little more heated, a little more seductive than it had ever felt before.

THE PLACE WAS PACKED, as it usually was. We'd paid the doorman and elbowed our way to the bar, ponying up to get a beer for Gareth and a vodka soda for me. I surveyed the scene as we waited. People were crammed in every part of the space, bodies moving together in time with the music. There were groups together, people clearly friends or more moving as a unit, but overall, everyone was one giant mass of heat and beat.

The beats pounding in my blood came from the DJ set up in the right front corner. An L-shape of turntables surrounded crates of records set on a small platform. A few DJs worked Heatwave, taking turns spinning their own sets off and on throughout the night, but it was all the same general vibe: old-school R&B, Soul, Funk, and Motown from the sixties and seventies blasting through the crowd. It was dance music with heart and heat, hence the name, I suppose. Music that echoed through time all the way down to people who hadn't even been born—whose parents might not have even been born—when those records had first come out. It didn't matter. These beats resonated through the decades, the transcendence of voice and horns and bass snaring everyone in the room. It was why I loved Heatwave so much—it felt fresh and alive, but time-less.

I favored darker music when working or listening on my own, more industrial, but I loved to dance here, to this music. I was swaying already, moving my wide hips in rhythm, when Gareth turned to me with my drink. He'd insisted on paying for it after I'd paid the small cover, and I had no problem letting him. I sipped my drink, a strong pour that made a delicious burn run down my throat, as Gareth took the time to look over the room himself. When his eyes came back to me, they snagged on where my body moved to the music, focusing in on my twisting hips for a long moment.

He leaned down to my ear. I knew his voice was loud, the puff of air at his words caressing my ear and making my gut clench, but it sounded like a whisper in the loud barroom when he said, "Dance with me."

Gareth extended his hand but waited for me to lead, for me to affirm and set the pace. I shoved my way through a pack of sweaty bodies to find a small space for us to stand, nearly chest to chest, and dance togeth-er.

We stood close, almost touching, moving separately to a driving Funk beat backed by blaring horns. Gareth eventually reached around to grab my hip. He rested his hand gently, almost reverently, there, not pulling me closer. I stepped in and pressed my hips to his until I felt a fist at my side, his hand grasping at the contact. I threw my hands up onto his shoulders and twisted my body to the music. We found our shared beat, our rhythm, quickly and moved together through the crush of bodies and the occasional pull of alcohol from our dangling cups. In the air, a different, more carnal, everyday human sort of magic hummed in the atmosphere.

WE DANCED FOR TWO hours, though there were breaks. Gareth and I had two more drinks each. He seemed fine, and I knew I was. Three drinks weren't enough to get me drunk, given the sweat and exertion from all the dancing. Enough for me to feel a little tipsy, a little giddy, but the sensations could also have been from the sparks continuing to rise between us. We'd make our way to the bar for breaks or snag water at the large cooler the bartenders kept filled. Or wade through the smokers on the back patio and chat for a few minutes in the cool breeze.

I'd long ago abandoned my jacket, tossed it on top of a counter in a darker corner of the dance floor. My body was slick with sweat and heated by other things as Gareth held me from behind. We swayed together to the music. I moved freely, my arms and hips and head waving to the sensuous pull of a more mellow R&B track. Gareth's arms were a steel band, moving with me but not against me, holding me but not inhibiting my movements. His hip movements echoed mine, close and steady, driving against, making my core clench and achy for more. I wanted to dance, to hold on to the anticipation and sweet build for longer, but I knew I'd give out soon. Partially because these last few hectic weeks had left me exhausted. Partially because I wanted Gareth to take me home, to my apartment, my bed, so we could get to the *more* before I was too tired.

I wanted to stretch it out as long as possible, so I pushed on, closing my eyes to block out the mass of people and the red glare of the dance lighting, and focus on what I felt in my body. For a time, I lost myself in the physical sensations, savoring each push and pull, each new rhythm we found together as the songs changed—all with closed eyes.

I enjoyed it until the new thrum in me went haywire, like a tuning fork slamming against a concrete wall. I tasted something metallic in my mouth, dark and unknown and not at all connected to the last vodka soda I'd downed twenty minutes before. A whisper, like a voice I recognized but did not fully know, talked a few rooms away, hitting my ears despite the noise level. My eyes popped open, and I saw a hazy vision hovering over the dance floor.

It was a man. Possibly. At least something shaped like a man. His dark eyes held stars and knowledge and an endless void that reminded me of my dream-meditation-vision. All I saw was him, his reclined body floating above, looking down, directly at me. He was shirtless but wore dark pants, his lithe muscles stark and glistening, his expanse of sandy skin on full display. His face was regal, hard yet playful, with full lips and a large, sharp nose. Those beautiful lips moved. His tongue shot out, and I couldn't tell if he was trying to say something or was licking his lips. His body was slightly out of focus, making specific details impossible.

Then I heard a voice, like an echo from a deep well, say, "Soon enough, sweetling." It wasn't outwardly threatening, but yet another unknown magical thing happening to me was terrifying. Who the hell was this dude or thing or whatever? Why was he looking at me? What type of magic was this? Most strangely, why did my body and the new thrum inside me want to respond, want to reach out and take him, hold him to me, connect with him?

Obviously, I'd stopped dancing, was trembling from the riot of feelings roaring in my body. He looked on for a few more beats, tilted his head in acknowledgment, and disappeared. I didn't take the time to think or talk.

I pushed my way through the hot, sweaty mass of dancers and ran right out the front door, my legs leading me to my apartment. Gareth followed close behind and questioned me as we made our way toward my apartment. I couldn't talk on the street, not until I knew I was safe in the wards of my building, locked away from whatever the thing had been, and free from the pull in my middle telling me to go back to him any way I could.

Fifteen

"IT WAS A GUY you'd never seen before, hovering above everyone on the dance floor?" Gareth asked for clarification after I'd explained why I had run away in the middle of our date.

I'd taken a large gulp of water, cooling myself from the drinks and the dancing and the frantic journey back to my apartment. Gareth stayed with me, taking my curt replies in silence until we reached my building. He followed me up, looked me over to make sure I was okay, then started in with the questions when we stood in the living room.

"Yeah," I said on a gasp after a big swallow. The cool water washed down, helped focus my attention, bringing a positive physical feeling I could narrow in on in my mind instead of my rapid heartbeat and the continual reverb from the thrum now firmly lodged in my middle.

"Did anyone else seem to notice?" he asked, his tone gentle but still pushing, as he tried to get as much info as he could.

I thought about it. No one else had acted as if they had seen the man, at least not that I remembered, so I shook my head no.

"Okay," he said, letting out a huffed breath and running a hand over his messy and damp blond hair. "Okay. Not so bad then."

"Not so bad?" I asked. "Some hot dude pops up out of thin air and is all... Ugh, I don't know, just ALL, and it's not so bad?"

"You thought he was hot?" he asked, sounding a little defensive.

"Not the point right now, Gareth."

He had the good grace to look sheepish at the reprimand and hang his head, though I saw a blush warring with a hard glint in his eyes as his face came back up toward mine. "Of course. You're right. Let me explain." He grabbed my hand and led me to my couch, and we sat facing each other, our knees grazing. Even with the shiver of fear of the unknown remaining, his touch sent a vibration of lust echoing through my body. Thankfully, the zing of lust helped me drown out the other odd feelings and emotions I had from the weird hovering-dude encounter. I focused on feeling, let it grow and run riot in my blood to help me chase away the other sensations I didn't quite understand.

"It could be any number of things. Like a spell placed on you, though with your protection charm, it would be hard to pull off. It could be some type of magical attack, but it's also unlikely. No other dancers seemed to see it. I hadn't seen it right in front of me, and I'd spot any other type of magic easily. Astral projection is the best explanation."

"Like projecting yourself through space?"

"Space or time, yes. Astral projection is possible. I've read many accounts of it, but I don't know anyone who could pull it off. Harley can't even do it, and she can do a lot more than the other mages I know."

"Explain it to me. Exactly."

"It works as any magic works on a fundamental level, through focusing power and intention. The difference is it takes an incredible amount of power and intention to pull it off, even for the brief span of time you said it lasted. To not only project your image but have the projection also relay feelings or emotions hints at a lot of power."

"You're not making it sound like a 'not bad' thing here," I whispered.

"No, no, no. Sorry. Lots of power doesn't necessarily mean a person is bad. Look at you. Lots of natural power with a good heart," he said with a genuine smile. "It's not so bad because astral projection has no actual effect on the world. It's a vision of sorts, directed at a particular person, but it has no physical correspondent." He looked over my shoulder for a minute and muttered, "There are accounts of more, of course. Very vague and performed by the most powerful and ancient of sorcerers, people able to move their physical selves with the same type of magic, but it's never been confirmed."

He offered a comforting look. "What you saw was intended for you, yes. Was a show of power, yes. I think it simply freaked you out because it's new to you. If you think about what it made you feel beyond the initial shock and fear, you may have a different opinion." He rested a hand on my knee and leaned in. "It has no physical power. It can't hurt you here on this plane. It may have been a warning of some sort, but it was nothing to fear in the moment."

"I'm a big coward then?" I groused.

"No. Of course not. You're brave, facing all this new magic and training with determination and grace." His face turned serious, pensive even. "I admire the hell out of you, Randy. Not because of your power but because of your bravery. The heart you show. It's a real thing of beauty."

It was my turn to blush, and as I did, I felt his hand move on mine, the whisper of his skin on mine. I tuned into the press of his knee, the small push an invitation of sorts. "We were having fun, weren't we? Until I ruined it with my freakout."

"First, don't worry about it. You did what you felt you needed to do to protect yourself in the moment. That is never a bad thing." He leaned in closer, a breath away from my face, and his voice dropped. "We were having a great time. At least I was, and I don't think we need to stop."

I wanted Gareth. Had for a while now. If I was being completely honest with myself, I wanted a different feeling to wash out the residual ickiness of fear of more unknowns entering the picture. There was enough in my life I didn't know, couldn't fully understand, and I didn't need to add "some guy astral projecting to me for a cryptic reason" to the long list. What I could understand, what felt familiar, was the pulse of lust growing more and more steady in my blood throughout the night. Gareth gave me the opening. I took it, to chase the feeling rather than focus on the more complex unknowns. Lust I knew, I liked, I could easily fall into and maybe even out of when needed. The other stuff, not so much.

Before I could fall, I needed to make sure Gareth was willing to take the same ride. Not that he wasn't attracted to me. I grew up a little too fat for the standard, so I'd become good at being able to tell when someone wanted me. Rejection, especially rejection because of my size, was never fun, so I played it safe. I did play, however, and liked it, so I also wasn't inexperienced.

What I was unsure of in the moment was Gareth's expectations. He seemed like a good guy, one I needed in my corner in more ways than one. We needed to have a chat before things went any further between us. "Gareth, there's a lot I'd like to do right now," I said, to soften any unintentional blow from me pulling away from him, putting space between us. "First, though, I have to be honest. I'm not exactly looking for a relationship. There's a whole lot going on, as you know. I don't think I could handle balancing a more committed, romantic thing along with all the rest."

Understanding shone in his eyes, but he also pulled back, so I needed to finish this. "Here's what I can give: friendship with some intimate benefits. I care for you, for your feelings, but I also know I need you to help me with training and magic and things. It could become a big, tangled mess if we tried to be more."

Gareth studied me a moment, his eyes sharp and knowing, but they softened after a beat. "I don't want to do anything to make you more stressed than you already are, Randy. There's a lot I'd like to do with you too. I'm fine with keeping it casual, based in friendship."

"To be clear, I don't want you to pine for me. To hope this becomes more. I can't tell the future. Not a magic power I have, yet at least. There are no guarantees. What I say I can give now is what you should expect. I don't want you to press me, but I also don't want you to get hurt."

"I'm a big boy, Randy. I'm also quite smart. I understand what you're saying, what you can give me, and I'll take whatever you can give."

I took him at his word and pushed forward, colliding with him, wrapping my arms around his broad back as my lips met his. Something like a growl sounded deep in his chest, and he surged upward, taking me in his arms and pulling me onto his lap as he leaned back on the arm of the couch, letting me take control of the kiss and ride it out, ride *him,* as I poured my moan into his mouth.

We clashed. It was hard and fast and fantastic. We nipped at each other, our tongues stroking, pushing, and retreating. We tasted each other, devouring until we both panted. I pulled back slightly to whisper gruffly, "All those things you want to do with me—tell me."

Gareth grunted as I ground down on his crotch to relieve the ache in mine. I went for his neck, kissing around the edges of his beard and sucking hard when a gasp slipped from his lips.

"You like to talk?" he asked in a hoarse whisper. I knew what he meant, and I licked my way up his neck before meeting his eye and nodding.

He grabbed my head and brought it down to give me another kiss, this one a little rougher, a little more forceful than the other. "Good to know," he said, a satisfied chuckle escaping.

He didn't talk. No. Instead, he wrapped a tight arm around my back and flipped us so we switched positions. I was now back to the couch, one of Gareth's arms wrapped around me, the other straight into the couch cushion, holding him up at an angle so he could slide a heated look up and down my body.

"Damn," he whispered and licked his lips, as if he were talking to himself. As if he couldn't help himself. His slightly feral smile was full of sex and promise when he met my eye again. He pulled his hand from around me and slid it from my waist down to tease the edge of my skirt. With his eyes never leaving mine, those eyes hard and wanting yet waiting, he asked, "May I?"

I nodded and gave my own deep chuckle. "Yes. So polite."

"Oh, what I'm going to do to you isn't going to be polite at all," he said as he slid his hand in, immediately moving over my panties and stroking the growing damp spot on the fabric. A hiss followed. "Goddamn. Already so wet. You wet for me, Randy?"

"Yes." I moaned as he shoved the side of my panties away and ran a large finger down the dripping, aching center of me.

"Good," he grunted, looking down at where his hand had disappeared up my skirt. "I'm going to play with you, make you writhe and moan for me here on this couch. Then, I'm going to lay you out and lick you until you scream for me. After all that, I'm going to take you slow and hard, make sure you feel every inch of me."

I was panting hard, shaking at his words and the wicked things his hand was doing. He dipped one finger inside me, pumping in and out slowly as his thumb hit the mark, circling my clit with steady pressure. I was half-gone already, my orgasm a shiny light at the end of a not-so-long tunnel, and he'd promised more. So much more. His words, his body, and the determination and lust on his face all told me he'd deliver on his promise too, so I ran toward my release.

I moaned for him. Writhed as he wanted me to do. I made incoherent sounds and whimpers, lifting my hips to meet the push and pull of his hand, the sweet release it promised. The whole while, he whispered to me about my smell, the taste of my sweat, the agony of not yet being inside me, and how much he wanted to drive into me but would make us both wait for it. It was the sweetest type of torture, until it wasn't. My climax barreled through me like a freight train, making my muscles strain and my voice cry out, arching me up off the couch with its intensity and force. Damn, it was good.

Gareth slowed but did not stop his hand until I'd come all the way down, was still and gasping for breath. He wore a smug, satisfied smile, the smile of a man who had just given a woman a fantastic orgasm and knew he could do it again too.

He stood from the couch, scooped me up in his arms, and gave me a sweet kiss. It was perfection, though I still wanted all he had promised me. "Want to finish this in your room?" he asked, not moving until I gave an agreement.

I opened my mouth to reply when a loud crash sounded from outside. My eyes rose in surprise as Gareth shouted a curse. He quickly laid me back on the couch and said, "Stay right there," as he ran toward my door.

The hell with that. I didn't know what was happening, but I wasn't about to lie there and not figure it out. It took me a second to get back up from the couch, so I was several beats behind him, getting to my apartment door as Gareth barreled out the outside entrance door. Then it hit me. The wards. It had to have been the wards; it was why Gareth had recognized the sound and acted immediately, but I'd had no clue. Once again.

I was more cautious going down the stairs because I wasn't stupid. It had to be the cult, and I was in no condition to confront them. However, I noticed DD hovering beside me. It'd thankfully vamoosed when Gareth and I had started kissing. I hadn't fully registered it, because… sexy times… until the black spot popped back up after their absence. Guess it knew to give us some privacy, which made me happy. I was equally glad DD had come back, shivering in my periphery, ready to help if needed.

When I slowly poked my head out from behind the doorway at the bottom, I found Gareth in the dimly lit lot, visibly seething as he slid a hand over a shimmering sigil about four feet from my door. "What happened?" I asked quietly.

He whirled around, concern in his eyes. "I thought I said to stay."

"I'm not a dog, Gareth," I said flippantly, stepping into the night after seeing the coast was clear.

He sighed and hunched his shoulders. "Sorry," he muttered. "Come here," he called, moving back to face the sigil.

I stood beside him and watched as he retraced the shimmery figure in the night and whispered some words in a language I didn't know. It flared a bright light, then disappeared as if never there. "This is the ward guarding your place," he said as he waved a hand at what had been there but was gone again. "I put it up the night we met."

"Yep. Remember all that."

"The wards block anyone out to harm you. Someone obviously showed up tonight to harm you. It repels and makes a metallic clanging sound to warn you as well. Likely made whoever scatter before I got down here. Sorry."

I stared at him for a moment. "You're sorry you made something which obviously does its job and protects me and my place?"

"No. You know what I mean. Sorry I couldn't catch whoever was down here."

"You were a little preoccupied," I mumbled.

"True."

"Look, Gareth. You're not my protector. I appreciate all your help with protection, but it's not your job, and you can't be everywhere at once, so no need to be sorry about anything."

He stared at me a moment, unblinking, his body locked tight, before he said, "Heard." I don't know what he heard though, how he took it in, but I intended for him to take it easy on himself, not get all short and rigid.

"Hey," I called, pulling him close, taking the big guy into my arms. "You helped. You really did. You aren't responsible for something shitty another person did, so I don't want you feeling bad about it."

He deflated, lowering his head so his forehead rested on mine before he let out a sigh. "I have my own issues, with thinking I can or can't protect people. From my past."

I could see it. Being unable to help those he cared for so long ago had probably done a real number on his psyche.

"I'm good. You're good. My place is good," I whispered. "No need to stress."

He pulled up and rubbed the back of his neck as he scanned the lot one last time. "Yeah. I suppose, but they could be back." He paused in thought. "Can I stay here tonight? Not to, you know, do anything. Don't know if I'd want to right now. I can sleep on the couch. I'd feel better if I were here with you."

I was more than fine with him staying because I'd also feel better with him at my place. "Sure. No problem. You can share my bed and get some non-sexy snuggles."

He cracked a smile. "I didn't really peg you as a snuggler."

"Psssht. Please. I'm a snuggle queen, which is good because it's all I can offer tonight. I'm exhausted from fear, adrenaline, dancing, and orgasms. Though, now that you mention pegging..."

Gareth barked out a laugh as he took my arm. "Definitely not on the agenda for tonight, but I wouldn't entirely rule it out," he said with a wink. It made me laugh–the banter, the easing of tension, the possibilities between us.

We went up to bed. Sleep took a while to come for both of us, even though we were exhausted. When it finally did, it was a deep, comfortable sleep with his big, tattooed arms wrapped around me tight.

Sixteen

THE NEXT MORNING WASN'T overly awkward. I joked. Gareth blushed a bit but acted kind and sweet—his usual self, really. Kind and sweet until he kissed me good-bye with so much heat, I was panting when he pulled himself away.

"Hate to leave like this," he said, his voice deeper, tinged with more gravel.

"We gotta do what we gotta do," I said, though I threw in a fake pout for good measure.

"True. The librarians can get huffy when I stroll in too late for special Sunday meetings."

"Wait. You work at the library?" I was a complete dolt. An insensitive jerk. I'd known him for weeks. He knew so much about me, and I knew no real facts about him other than he was a mage who trained with Harley and had a traumatic intro to magic. I knew who he was from our time together, but not too many of the basics. The first-date type things I probably should've known since we'd had sex and all. "I'm so sorry," I said, ashamed of myself. "I'm such an ass for not knowing."

He cocked his head, concern clear in his face when he said, "It's perfectly all right, Randy. You've had a lot going on these last few weeks."

"Not an excuse. Tell me, in the two minutes you have, what it is you do exactly."

He laughed and said, "I'm a special collections librarian at the university."

I let out a whistle. "Mr. Fancy Pants over here. Got to say, never knew a librarian like you when I was in school."

He pulled me close and placed a quick, sweet kiss on my forehead as he said, "You've never met anyone like me at all."

I laughed, playfully smacking his chest as I pulled away. "Yeah, yeah. Big talk, big guy."

He gave me a wink and a squeeze of my hand, and he was out the door, off to his meeting about fancy books.

I, sadly, didn't have the day off. One of my scheduled employees needed the afternoon for a family thing, so I was taking her place on the schedule, slinging coffee and baked goods for a few hours over the lunch shift. At least there'd be tasty coffee literally on tap to help me get through it, and the baking I'd need to get done later in the day.

###

It was during a lull, the sweet spot on Sunday afternoon between one thirty and two o'clock, when the lunch rush was over and the end-of-day crunch began. Merry and Mia popped in, knowing the ebb and flow of business in Warm Regards almost as well as I did at this point. Without shame, I put them to work restocking so we could take care of the few customers in line. They stayed behind the counter to tease me, along with my assistant manager, Deb.

"There was a shiny black motorcycle out back when I took the morning trash out," she called, a smile in her voice.

Merry and Mia turned to gape at me. I tried to pretend I didn't hear anything as I arranged cookies in the display case. Someone smacked my shoulder, and I whipped my head around and saw Merry standing there, a bright smile on her face.

"Would it be Gareth's shiny black motorcycle?" Mia asked.

"Possibly," I muttered but then threw them a wicked smile.

"Who's Gareth? He the hottie who comes in here for you sometimes?" Deb asked.

"Yep," Merry said. "He's very much into Randy. He's also very sweet, so I like him for you."

"Thanks, sis," I said, giving her a quick sideways hug, "but it's not serious or anything. It's all very casual."

"Surprise, surprise," Mia said.

"And what's that supposed to mean?"

"It means, since Assface McGee, you've kept everything casual."

"And what of it," I called back, defensive at her tone and the general callout.

"It's totally fine, Randy," Merry soothed. "You're free to explore your sexuality however you see fit. No one should judge you for it." She then turned hard eyes on our little sister pointedly.

"I'm not judging her," Mia whined. No one liked to upset Merry. "All I'm saying is it's been years, and she's dated around but hasn't wanted to do more. Before He-Who-Is-A-Dipshit, she played around, sure, but also had longer-term relationships."

Merry looked back at me to say something else. Whether in support or rebuttal, I'd never really know, because Deb noticed the person waiting at the register who we all had failed to see walk up in our apparent need to air sister laundry for the entire world to hear.

"So sorry, ma'am. What can I help you with?"

"Bless your heart for finally noticing me, but I came to have a word with your owner there." The voice, and the light giggle punctuating her words, made my blood run cold. I'd never forget it, and here it was in Warm Regards, in the middle of a sunny Sunday afternoon. The voice and giggle belonged to the lady who had been giving orders the night Starry Wisdom had almost kidnapped me.

I turned her way slowly, panic and fear screaming in my veins, and saw the petite blonde smirking. In any other circumstance, I might say she looked cute as a button: platinum-blonde hair in a sleek flipped-up bob with a red headband pulling the hair from her face, which was a flawless pale ivory. A hint of makeup accentuated her pert lips, button nose, and high-but-not-too-high prominent cheekbones. Her dress was a simple black sheath over her slim body, a belt the same crimson shade as her headband, the only piece to break up all the black. She was a classic beauty, or at least a twentieth-century American classic beauty. She could have been in a café in the 1960s or in the 2010s, and she'd fit seamlessly in either.

Her eyes gave away the beautiful disguise, or at least pointed to the evil hiding under all the pretty. They were a crystalline blue, like an ice storm stretched across the horizon. A blizzard rolling in to do real damage regardless of what was in its way. She also didn't blink. Not once, the entire time she was in my place. It was unnerving. Add the shimmery glow of sigils marking all parts of her exposed skin, a glow I could see because of my new training, and it all spelled something very not good.

Deb looked perplexed, but Merry and Mia stiffened, as they were more attuned to the shifts in my mood from years of sharing space—and the occasional bedroom, which was a totally different type of nightmare I'd rather not remember. They gawked at the woman, who slid over from the customer line to face me from the opposite side of the food case.

"Good to meet you face-to-face, Miranda."

The name drop was clue number two to my sisters. I hated people calling me Miranda. No one who knew me more than a few minutes did so unless they were clueless or mean, and it made my sisters crowd in on either side of me.

All the while, DD hovered in the usual spot, though it started shaking more violently the moment the woman spoke.

"Well, isn't this nice? All the Carter sisters together. Y'all are so sweet, helping your big sister with her"—she rolled her hand in the air, a clear sign of distaste on her face—"little shop."

"How are you here?" I asked through gritted teeth, doing my best to maintain focus so I could let loose if she tried to attack.

"First." She smiled faintly and snapped her fingers. The sounds of the café became muffled, as if I was hearing the bustle from one room over. "Much better. No need for everyone to hear what we say. You may have no problem spreading your sordid business all around, but I prefer to be more discreet."

"What are you doing here?" I was seething.

Mia and Merry huddled closer. Merry grabbed my hand in hers, and I could feel her shaking. It was enough to make me more bold, more protective.

"Actually, don't care. Get the fuck out, if you know what's good for you."

"Oh, hon, I'm not here to harm you or anyone else. What with the wards and all, I couldn't get in if that were the case."

Surprise must have shown on my face, because she let out a tinkle of laughter.

"Sweetie, really, you should be better informed. You're like a little babe in the woods." Her smirk was lethal. "Let me explain slowly. The wards your man put up around your shop? They are specific. Any ward placed in a physical space must be precise. Because he couldn't rightly put a ward up to block out everyone, as this is a business where people come and go, he placed a ward to block out any entity with ill intent."

"How do you know what Gareth did?" Mia barked out before I sliced my eyes her way and shook my head gently. She needed to stay clear of this woman and not let her smart mouth get her in trouble.

"Why, I tested it last night, of course."

Merry and Mia started. I seethed. "The ward went off last night because of you."

"Yes, and, honey, I am sorry for interrupting your little date, but really, if you ask me, you should be thankful. It's unseemly, doing such things with a man you barely even know."

I had enough. "Get out."

"I will. Promise. Only wanted to introduce myself formally. My name is Macy. A pleasure to meet you, Miranda." She raised her hand, and I wasn't taking any chances. I put a DD shield between her and my sisters. It became a literal shield, a floating disk hovering between us and her. I blinked in surprise because I had made no sigil, muttered no spell to get the effect. I simply thought, and it was. A first for me. She didn't notice my surprise but acted amused by my magical display.

"Nice trick," she said, her voice dripping in condescension. "Though, a basic trick. Not real power. That's what I wanted to talk to you about, sugar. Real power. What you have, what we could unleash, what we could make of the world. Together, as powerful women."

"No thanks. Not really into kidnapping and murder," I said with a fake smile.

"All means to a glorious end, I assure you."

"An end where gods wreak havoc on the earth?" Mia asked, and this time I pinched her side. She needed to keep quiet.

Macy put her cold gaze on my sister as if contemplating her truly for the first time, and my hackles rose.

"Over here," I said, snapping my fingers at her. "You're talking to me, remember?"

"There's so much I could teach you," she said once she turned back to me.

"Already have plenty of tutoring lessons."

"They don't know all you are. All you could be. I can help you harness all your darkness, bend it to your will, direct it in a way it needs to be directed."

"Doing just fine as of now, not being tied up like a sacrificial lamb, so forgive me if I don't jump at your offer," I spat back at her, though the direction she was taking called back to my worries about my powers.

She seemed to offer answers about the source of my powers, though from her, I couldn't trust anything to be true. Couldn't trust she would tell me any type of truth.

She held my gaze for long moments, her eyes piercing through the haze of the DD shield. "Take your time. Think on it. You're a smart girl. You may change your mind and stop hanging out with riffraff. It'd be better for you and them. Your sisters... Well, I don't rightly know how well those others could protect them if someone were to come after them."

"Leave, bitch," I commanded, rage filling me at her threat to Merry and Mia.

She laughed her tinkle laugh. "No need for name calling, darling. Simply offering you options. Every girl needs options."

Before I could give another snarky reply, she turned on her heels and strolled out the door, her perfect hair swaying as she bounced away.

The din of the café rushed back. Deb looked confused and a little rattled, and Mia breathed out. "Who was the preppy from hell?"

I didn't answer her, to focused on what needed to happen next. "I have to call Harley. Now."

"AND THEN, SHE STARED at Mia. Right at Mia, like she was something to study, to know more about. Nope. Nuh uh. Not happening."

I was in mid-tirade, Harley and Gareth off to the side as I paced the length of my living room. They'd got there quick, so I'd hurried them upstairs. No need for even more weirdness to go down in my place of business. Merry had soothed my manager, deflected her questions with her sweetness and a conversation about Deb's foster animals, but I'd wanted to keep my employees and my customers as far away from this crap as possible. Hell, I wish I were as far away from this crap as possible, but no such luck for me. Or my sisters. They kept getting caught in the crossfire, which I did not appreciate.

"Breathe," Gareth said in an effort at calming me, I'm sure. It only made me more irate.

"I am breathing. Wouldn't be walking around alive if I wasn't," I snapped back before I rounded, wild-eyed, at Harley. "I'm done. They've come after me a few times now. I can't let it happen again, them catching me by surprise, putting other people in danger. We need to act."

"Out with it, girl. What do you want?" Harley said.

"I want to attack. No more waiting. I want to know your plan to take them down, and I want to go for it."

Gareth snapped his shoulders back, stiffening at my newfound offensive position. Harley... Well, Harley smiled and agreed without saying anything, more than ready to go after Starry Wisdom with whatever we had.

Seventeen

HARLEY'S PLAN WAS SIMPLE. Attack.

Just joking. It involved many moving pieces and complex magic, more recon, and more training, but the gist of it boiled down to attacking. The when and how of it was more convoluted. She needed to find out more about the wards and spells around the church, think on how to negate any power the structure potentially held. She figured the cult drew a lot from the church itself, as it always popped up whenever they were causing a ruckus somewhere. Getting rid of the thing could make the cultists more vulnerable, easier to take out.

I didn't care about theories or specifics. After Macy had shown up at the café, I'd felt angry, then sad and dejected, then angry all over again. It was my home, literally and figuratively, and she'd dirtied it up with her presence.

Was part of me tempted by Macy's offer? Not at all. Not even a little. I didn't want power over people. I have no grand schemes to become some sort of magical overlord or anything. Maybe people would think my dreams small, but they were my dreams, my goals, and they all rested in Warm Regards. All I wanted was to make tasty treats people loved, and to take care of my family. Maybe have the occasional sexy romp with a hot dude, like Gareth for instance. I didn't need, or really want, anything else.

Macy and her evil cult threatened all of it: my business, my baking, my family, and my fun. Even if those ambitions were small, they were mine, and I'd hold tight to them, protect them at all costs. So, yeah, I was ready to follow whatever Harley said to end this, so I could go back to my regularly scheduled reality.

THE FIRST THING HARLEY mandated was more internal shadow work, though she wanted to supervise. After the weird session I'd had on my own, and her freakout about it, I had no objections to this. Even sacrificed my mornings for it. Every day I'd go to Harley's and work in her gym area while she kept an eye on me from her office, researching and planning. I didn't create an anchor like she'd suggested before because it took a lot of time and practice. She figured being around would work well enough for the moment, until we got over the Starry Wisdom mess and had time to figure out what thing we could use to effectively tether me to this plane.

The first day was enlightening. I did self-meditation and ended up in my kitchen again, but no massive inky entity takeover. I did still see my reflection with the black eyes. Other-Randy simply studied me, as if waiting. Apparently, it was my move now.

When I dipped out of my meditation, I explained it all to Harley. She asked, "Have you tried to use your power since your meditation experience?"

"I threw up a shield with DD between my sisters and Macy at the shop yesterday. I think that's about it."

"No sigil or spell?"

"Nope," I said, still finding it odd myself.

"What's DD?" she asked.

"Oh, yeah. Um, it's what I call the Deep Dark. Seemed better since it's constantly around and all," I said with a head tilt toward the ever-present ball of shadow beside me. It shook in a way I thought of as expressing happiness. Maybe I was projecting, but I felt like the more time I spent with it and the more I acknowledged it, the more I came to understand it. Like the more connected I became with it. I imagined its feelings, or maybe I actually understood its expression of feelings. I didn't know how I'd be able to tell either way, so I didn't linger too long on the fact.

Harley snorted but continued with her original line of thought. "The vivid internal exploration you experienced days ago may have led to some form of unleashing of power. The shielding, as you call it, isn't too far off from the spell and sigil you learned earlier, the one you used against the men threatening you and your sister in the parking garage. However, it is different and should've required a sigil and spell to work on your end."

"I shouldn't have been able to do the shield?"

"Not like you did. It's a very advanced wielding skill, Randy," Harley said with her usual blunt tone, though there was a cautious softness there, as if she didn't want to freak me out too much. I mean, I was already pretty freaked by everything, so I got it. "Sigils help focus and intention. It takes decades upon decades of practice to maintain the proper spell without the physical marker of its focus and intention. I can only do it with a handful of spells and wards."

"There was nothing I said along with it," I admitted. "I thought of a shield, asked DD to do it in my mind, I guess, and bam. There it was, a little shield of Deep Dark between us and Macy."

She considered all I told her. "The Deep Dark flocks to you. You attracted it before you even began wielding magic. Add that to your power's overall connection to shadow and darkness and your recent vision, you may well be much more advanced than we even realized. Let's test it," she muttered as she strolled down the length of the gym area.

I watched her closely. I wasn't stupid. Her version of testing likely meant some type of surprise attack.

I wasn't wrong. Harley spun around, a sigil on her hand flaring as she flung some type of magic out toward me. Wind whooshed through the space and slammed into DD, which I'd flung up as a shield. I flinched, but the force didn't hurt me. Didn't even touch me, actually.

"Interesting," she said, coming forward to examine the thin, see-through layer of DD extended in front of me. "What did you think about when I attacked?"

"I thought I needed a shield."

"It followed your call, with little effort on your end. I'm sure the focusing exercises helped, but it seems you've moved beyond needing sigils to create an effect, particularly with the Deep Dark. Let's see if you can run it through its paces."

We went through the spells I already knew, all the ways I already could get DD to do certain things, only without me using sigils or words. I thought, and it happened.

"Now, try something new," Harley commanded.

"Like what?"

"Like anything you can think of to have the Deep Dark perform for you," she replied.

I thought about it. First thing I thought of was light. Or the idea I could probably block out light. I held the intention in my mind and DD shot off, splitting into two so it could engulf the two hanging lights in the gym space.

The room dimmed and Harley said, "Nicely done."

With the room dimmed, the shadows were longer, so I tried another idea. I moved close to a shadow along the wall, thought of what I wanted, and DD delivered. Harley whistled at the results.

"I can't even see you. It's like you did an advanced cloaking spell."

Inside the now-extended shadow, DD practically purred along my skin as I gave it a mental nudge of thanks.

"All good for hiding and recon, but think of offense too."

Honestly, I'd been avoiding that. I had no real problem hurting someone trying to hurt me or mine, but going into the fight first made my stomach do a funny flip. I was also thinking of DD more and more as a being, which made it hard for me to use it as a weapon.

I had an odd flash of thought out of nowhere. In my mind, I saw a long spear, black as the deepest, darkest chocolate, with a wicked blade at the top. Why it came to mind, I didn't know, but it was what popped into my head when I thought about fighting.

"Impressive," Harley said. "Though I don't think Gareth or I know much about spears. This is something you'll have to work with on your own. What can you do with it now?"

I tested the weight of it in my hand. It was sturdy, though it had the shimmery quake of DD I was accustomed to at this point. It was about my height, so not the best for fighting up close, though there was a nice groove in the handle about a foot down from the blade, which might be handy. What I knew was I could throw it. Whether I could throw it well was another story.

I squared up, pulled back, and aimed for the far wall. The spear clattered loudly to the ground about five feet away from me, after taking an immediate nosedive. I laughed and said, "Looks like I'll need practice."

"True, but also, think about it. Don't simply physically throw the thing, put your intention behind it as well. It's a magical weapon, after all."

Made sense, so I did. It hovered abnormally long in the air, slowly making its way toward my intended target, despite gravity. It was funny looking, and I'd been so stressed, I laughed at this absurd scene: a sharp weapon wobbling like it was drunk, creeping toward a wall.

Harley even chuckled a bit, and with my focus smashed, the DD spear crashed to the ground once again before contracting back into a small, dense blackness and shooting back to the rest of the DD at my side.

Harley came up to pat my back. "Not bad for a first timer, but you'll need work. Use your new practice space at home for this. It'll be less dangerous for you to do on your own. You can also work on getting the Deep Dark to do other things. It's a muscle, so work it, even with mundane tasks."

I nodded and blew out a breath. More work, more practice... but it was necessary to get rid of Starry Wisdom. "Does all this mean the meditation-vision thing I experienced had some effect?"

"I think it did. My suspicion is you unconsciously disconnected yourself from your internal power a long time ago, probably when you first started to actively repress it as a kid. The vision was your brain processing the internal work it had to do to bridge your power with your conscious activity."

"My mind playing tricks on me," I muttered.

"They like to do that sometimes," Harley said. "It's a good thing. This will help us when we confront Starry Wisdom."

How much it could help, though, and how ready I was to help remained to be seen.

WHAT COULD I SAY? Sometimes I truly was an idiot. In this instance, I was an idiot because the more I thought about my power, what it might do, the more I thought about how it would react at the black church and what it might mean. Which meant I eventually went there on my own, to see if the feeling changed, since my vision had somehow connected me back to whatever magic lived inside me in a more concrete way. I headed there later the same afternoon, after doing some baking and mulling over my options. I was still nervous about what my powers could do, what it all might mean, and no one had answers for me. Exploring it on my own, at least a little, seemed like a good call.

I rolled up a few blocks from the church on a shady side street, close enough to get there and back quickly in case I needed to make a run for it. I didn't want to get right up on it or anything, only close enough to it to see if I felt anything.

Didn't take me long before I found out. When a break in houses revealed a sliver of the black steeple against the afternoon sky, my insides thrummed harder. My internal string resonated, making goose bumps pop up all over my body. Obviously, the feeling was still there. Not only there, but much more intense and visceral.

I'd like to think I was calling the shots, but I couldn't tell. Not really. What I did know was I moved closer to the church, and before I'd realized it, I was at the wrought-iron gate surrounding the thing. Blinked and was there. I didn't think I'd teleported or anything. I thought I had been so focused on the feeling, I'd made my way there subconsciously. It didn't feel great.

A quick look around told me I was alone, no cultists in sight, though I knew they could lurk in any shadow ready to snatch me up. I didn't need to be there. But I couldn't help myself. I walked through the scrolled wrought-iron fence and up the stone walkway to lay my hands on the actual building.

The thrum was feverish, vibrating at a frequency so strong, it took over my thoughts. I needed to touch it, to feel it, and to go inside and see, to know. I reached a hand forward, noting the building was made from black wood. Not wood painted black but black wood. Wood like I'd never seen before. Wood, I knew in my gut, didn't belong in this world.

I still touched it, almost like something inside compelled me on, even as my mind told me to turn and run. When I gave in to the compulsion and touched the ominous black doors, the same roar I had heard the first night here spilled into the quiet day, loud, long, and lingering. I felt it in my bones, the sad, pleading call. It was the yell of a wild animal in need, though it was not like any animal I'd ever heard in my life. It was deeper, darker, more terrifying. Scary, though a part of me was acting drawn to it instead of being repelled by it. The sound jarred my senses enough it returned the thrum so I could process what was happening around me. I noticed the fevered quaking of DD at my side, then looked even farther out, realizing how exposed I was and how much shit I'd be in if some cultist strolled up.

I heard the horribly sad and terrifying dark keen echoing behind me as I bolted for my car. My experiment had given me some new information, sure, but it wasn't exactly comforting to know.

EIGHTEEN

PROPERLY FREAKED OUT, I hid in my apartment for the rest of the night. Maybe I should have practiced with DD on my own, as Harley had suggested, but things were sort of crashing in on me. I needed a mental health break, which meant cookies in front of the TV while I watched one of my comfort shows. Usually, it would be Buffy, but I couldn't deal with vampire slaying and demon fighting right now. Veronica Mars it was.

Eventually I ended up crashing on my couch, Veronica's snark a nice lullaby after a rough few weeks. Don't know how or when it had happened, only knew it did because I was suddenly in a dream.

How did I know it was a dream? I was back at the black church, and I was wearing a dark robe. Not like the hooded cult roes but like a toga, one so dark it seemed made from shadows. Barefoot, I stepped up to the open door, curious where this dream would lead, though the smoke-like puff of DD rising from under my step felt like a warning of some type. A warning I ignored.

The enormous doors slammed closed behind me, the sound of a lock clicking in place loud as a shot through the silent room. Dark, otherworldly wood covered the inside of the church. The walls, the floors, and the lines of pews were made from the stuff, a wood so black it felt like a void. Definitely felt like it was unnatural, to my world at least. I reached out to stroke a straight-backed pew when I noticed I was hazy. As in, my hand was slightly see-through, like I was a shadow myself. Or a shade walking the church. I could still feel things though, touch them, sense them all around me, so I stroked the gleaming blackness of the wooden pew.

It was rougher than I had imagined, chipped and scarred from something whittling away at it. I jerked back with a hiss when a splinter lodged in my finger, causing the finger, then my entire hand, to throb in pain. I inspected the wound, a small thing to cause so much havoc, and saw a black barb neatly embedded, a sliver of otherworldly darkness stuck into my quasi-translucent finger. I stuck it in my mouth to suck. A bad habit, I know, but still a habit whenever I hurt my hand. The pastry instructors had got real mad about it, but I still never shook it off. When my finger touched my tongue, however, it was like I'd licked a live wire. An unpleasant jolt, one with an acrid taste, tore through my mouth, down my throat, and deep into the pit of my stomach. I stumbled back, my body thrown off by the sensation,. I may have even gagged a little as I stared back down at the tiny speck of wood lodged firmly in my finger. Not good at all.

The roar sounded again. Inside the church, it was obvious it had come from the steeple. The church itself, however, was one large room, mostly filled with pews, except for a small, raised altar front and center where the pews faced. No doors were obvious. Not even a bathroom, which I mean, come on. Bathrooms needed to be handy in any place.

It wasn't until I made it to the altar when I noticed the small door behind it. There weren't normal door locks on it but chains, big old metal manacle-looking things woven through four metal loops on each side and pulled tight across the door. The end wasn't locked. It looked welded together. Whatever was in there, Starry Wisdom did not want it out. With it screaming in a mournful and angry way, I shivered to think of what the creature could be and what it could do. I moved toward it, most definitely feeling a need to get closer, but I didn't know if it was a good or bad thing, and in this new world of magic and monsters, I couldn't be too careful.

Another roar called, guttural and enticing, the bass in it so booming, it made the chains across the door rattle along with it. My insides thrummed harder in response, and the pulse of my hurt finger intensified, spreading up into my wrist and forearm.

I slowly backed away, fighting the pull of the keening—the pull of whatever the thing was behind the door. However, a second rattle sounded, and I whipped my head around and saw the tall black church doors shuddering, as if taking a blow from the outside. Someone or something was trying to get in, and I was stuck between two doors rattling against their locks. A purr, somewhat animal and somewhat not but 100 percent inhuman, echoed in the chamber. Then a laugh, sharp and cold but not edged with viciousness or danger, sounded. Finally, words. "Sweetling" filled the space to bursting, skittering over my skin in a passionate caress. "Soon," it promised.

I came awake to Veronica and Logan in a clinch on my TV screen, nervous sweat licking my skin and a throb in my hand, the visible bite of the black splinter from my dream causing a very real ache.

MY ARM CONTINUED TO hurt like hell, all the way up to my elbow, even though I'd quickly removed the splinter when I had awakened from my dream.

The pain made it hard to work, and I needed to make croissants, which required rolling, turning, rolling, and turning, over and over to get the right amount of lamination. Not good with an achy arm.

Even less good was the realization splinter and the arm pain meant my dream had somehow merged with reality. I brooded over this newfound power or magical manipulation. No idea which.

When I finished baking, I went to Harley, handed her the splinter in a baggie, and told her what had happened.

"You dream-walked," she explained.

"What?"

"It's a rare gift with mages, but I've known a few who can do it, including Gareth. Means you can physically step into or out of dreams."

"How does that even work? Dreams aren't real."

"Some are mental manifestations, true. Some, though, are prophecy or omen or interaction with another plane of existence. In those cases, dream-walking is possible. Usually takes a lot of knowledge, power, and practice, but again, you're doing it without even trying."

She cocked her head, studying me like I was something to figure out. She'd done it before, but it bugged me today. "Stop looking at me like I'm some puzzle you need to solve," I barked. "I'm a person."

"Solving you would help you out, you know."

Damn it, I hated Harley was so often right, so I ignored the poke. "What about the wood sliver thing?" I asked instead, pointing at the small sliver of the awful wood from the church building.

She looked at it more closely. "I may need to call in a favor from a friend, someone who knows more about interdimensional objects, to have a look at this."

"It felt off, like it wasn't natural. You think it really isn't... like, not of this world?"

"Not of this plane at least, but like I said, I need confirmation. Either way, knowing more about the structure of the church might be the edge we need to take it down."

"Burning it to the ground might be helpful too."

"We can't burn it. It pops up in different places again and again, after lots of destruction. Something about it allows it to travel across space and time. We need to figure it out, stop it from being able to disappear and reappear at will. No reappearing black church might mean no more Starry Wisdom."

Made sense. Someone or something had built the black structure with interdimensional magic mojo or whatever, and it helped the cult fill up its magical battery, so to speak.

"Keep an eye on that," Harley said, nodding toward my arm, which I was cradling almost unconsciously because of the persistent ache. "If it gets worse, let me know. I'll be sure to ask my friend about it too. I'll look into it some, cross-reference my books for any mention of dream-walking injuries."

I gave her a chin lift in silent thanks but was done—done with the conversation and the worry and finding out even more new-and-improved magical feats I could unwittingly perform. I needed a break and some sleep, but sleep seemed far too dangerous. Maybe I'd have to pull a Nancy à la *Nightmare on Elm Street*—stay awake if possible. Not fun in the slightest. Maybe a chat with Gareth would help.

GARETH AND I HAD texted back and forth since the night he'd slept over a few days ago. It wasn't awkward, thankfully. We seemed to fit nicely into a friendly groove. A friendly-but-sexually-charged groove. We'd even had one fight-training session since then, but Gareth had been a perfect gentleman at the gym. I'd been sly, more touchy, more open, but he either hadn't picked up my signals or had ignored them, because nothing had come from our one-hour fight fest.

Now, I needed him for information, for real talk about real experiences, so all the more reason to be casual with Gareth. True, if we became something more, he would help me. The fear was whether or not he would continue to help me if something official between us ended. I was too new, too wary of my magic, too dependent. It might make me stay in a relationship when I shouldn't, or make him pull away if we ended things. Neither were great options, hence the friends-with-benefits distinction. It might be a waste—everything might still blow up—but it wouldn't be because I hadn't been up front about how I felt and what I could give.

It was a lot on top of a lot doubled up with a lot, so I tried to push it out of my mind. I was a grown-ass woman. He was a grown-ass man. We had come to an agreement about where we stood, and I needed to not worry about it. I called and asked to meet up with him, and he agreed.

As soon as he strolled into my apartment, as I was shutting the door behind him, I started. "I heard from a little bird you can dream-walk?"

He spun around, surprise clear on his face, and said, "Why would Harley tell you I'm a dream-walker?"

I waved my still-sore arm at him, then told him all about my dream, just as I'd told Harley. I ended with saying, "She told me it was one form of magic she couldn't perform but you could."

He nodded. "True. With all forms of magic, there's a small amount of affinity or natural ability involved. For certain forms of magic, like dream-walking, it's crucial. Humans can't shove their way into dreams with intent, knowledge, and power. There has to be something there to help bridge the gap."

"What thing?"

"I hate to say it, because I'm sure you're sick of hearing it in relation to your power, but no one knows for sure. Best theories say an individual must gain equal attunement between body and mind while also having an affinity for scrying—reading signs of the future in objects."

"You can read the future?"

"Not quite. It's more of a guess, intuition mixed with knowledge, affinity, and magical power."

"Have you done any scrying about me?"

He nodded but didn't elaborate. I normally wouldn't push, but it was specifically about me, so I felt entitled.

"What'd you find?"

He sighed. "Nothing concrete. Only darkness and growing power."

"Sounds ominous."

"Not necessarily. You already have darkness around you, and your power continues to grow, which is why it wasn't much. There was someone else there, something else connected to you I couldn't figure out, but it was beyond old and filled with even more power. It was with you, not threatening, so it read as a positive."

I had no idea what it could mean or how I should even feel about the vague, ominous nature of what he said, so I simply nodded.

"Okay, back on topic. This dream-walking stuff wasn't the most fun, so should I be worried?"

"You should always be cautious, Randy," Gareth said, taking my hand. "However, much of what you fear, outside the cult, centers on you and your own abilities. Exploring it more, with some knowledge at hand, might be a good thing."

"I simply go with the flow and see what happens?"

Gareth shrugged. "In this case, I don't think it would hurt."

I held up my sore hand, and he shook his head.

"Much."

I wasn't convinced, but like everything else in my life over the last several weeks, I needed more time and knowledge to make a better decision. Gareth said he'd bring me some books on dream-walking, so more studying was in order.

He had to be somewhere, so he excused himself. As he headed for the door, I stopped him.

"When are we going to go out again?" I asked casually from the couch.

He slowly turned toward me, his smile growing sexy, and drawled, "Whenever you want."

"I want."

A dark, masculine chuckle sounded, and he replied. "I know. As do I, Randy. As do I. How about dinner, two days from now?"

"Perfection," I said with a wide smile pulling on my face.

He waved and strolled out, leaving me wondering about dreams and dinner plans.

Nineteen

GARETH DROPPED OFF BOOKS on dream-walking the following day with a sweet kiss and instructions of a sort. "Remember, a lot of this is theoretical. No one knows definitively what dream-walking is or how it works. All they know are best practices and the people most likely to do it."

"'Don't get your hopes up,'" I said in a deep-voiced impersonation of Gareth, which made me chuckle and made him give a small smile. "Got it."

I spent a few days reading, occasionally texting Gareth with questions here and there. It was a lot to go over, and honestly, I did a bunch of skimming because so much of it was leading up on how to do something I, once again, could do without knowing how. I'd likely need those process steps later, but for now, the fear of another random dream-walk made me focus more on what it was and what could happen.

Gareth had been mostly right. No one person, at least in the books I now had, gave a definitive answer about what it was. They did, however, all have fairly common answers, with a few specifics tweaked here and there. Overall, dream-walking connected with prophetic abilities or affinities in one way or another. Dream-walking, after lots of specific and in-depth prep work, usually helped someone dig deeper into the past or give hints about the future.

Mine didn't feel like past or future visions. I couldn't place it, but my dream was current, like maybe it was real time—or at least close to it. It felt like I was there, in the space I knew to be there, at this point in time. The dream I'd walked through was less a dream and more a reflection of reality, like the shadow plane. I didn't find any talk of that kind of thing, so specifics for my case reached a dead end.

What all the reading had done, however, was ease my mind a little. Gareth's talk had helped, too. A lot of my anxiety stemmed from not trusting my powers. I needed to connect with and learn to trust the thrum buried deep inside of me. It could guide me so I could let it. Maybe a dream world was the best place to let it happen, as long as I didn't touch any more weird wood while I was taking a walk through dreams like I was Sandman or something.

I read, I thought, and I tried to meditate and connect more, though I didn't do any more vision-quest-like things on my own. Simply tried to stay quiet and comfortable with myself, exist in myself, connected to all parts of myself, attempting to bridge who I had thought I was for so long with all the new magic and power I felt crashing around inside me now. Meditation calmed me, eased my fears. Enough so I figured if I found myself in the dream-walking world again, put back at the black church, I'd take the opportunity to see what I might discover.

DURING ALL OF THIS, the monthly Carter Skype Session took place. I'd been able to bow out the previous month, acting like I was sick to avoid everyone. Merry and Mia knew the truth, so they weren't letting me out of it with vague or concrete excuses. However, they had agreed Mom and Dad didn't need to know anything about the mess going on in Columbus. If they did, the Carter parents would be in their car in a flash, ready to defend us from whatever cults or monsters might come our way. It was lovely we had them but also terrifying to think about them caught up in this danger, so avoidance was key.

I was glad once we were in it to be back in the group Skype. Merry, Mia, and I huddled around Mia's huge computer setup because it was the best. Mia had literally laughed at my little Dell and complained, frequently, about the tech she was "forced to endure" whenever she helped the kids at Merry's nonprofit, due to the lack of funds.

It was always the same, and there was comfort in the familiarity. The three daughters sitting together in one apartment, Mom and Dad hunched over their laptop. Mia had insisted on giving them the gear and setting all of it up for them soon after they had moved down, so it was better than mine and Merry's. We snacked and chatted and always ended up playing some type of game.

This time it was an old classic: hangman. We'd pick a phrase, and Mom and Dad would try to get it. Then vice versa. We went through a few rounds and were in stitches when we miserably failed to guess the phrase "All that jazz."

"I mean, really, girls. The number of times I played *Chicago* for you..." Mom tsk-tsked at us in a teasing voice. She was one for show tunes. Hell, we had even watched *Chicago* together live at the Ohio Theatre a few years ago.

"It's shameful, Marie," Dad said with a grin.

Merry pouted, Mia slumped in her chair and whined, and I sat back for a moment so struck by the normalcy and love of it, this weird technological moment allowing us to connect despite evil cults and magic and distance. I missed my parents often, but doing this helped, and I needed to store up the warmth and love in such moments, hold on to it, store it away in my mind to remember when other things felt like they were scary and new and unknown. This, the Carters having a ridiculously good time, was what could anchor me, no matter what.

Mom was astute. Tuned in to her girls, much like Merry. It was where Merry got it from, really. Of course, she noticed me thinking quietly in the moment, so she jumped on it.

To be honest, the surprise was it had taken her this long to bring it up. We'd chatted several times over the weeks since I was first thrown into the world of the occult. Each time, she'd picked up on something off in my voice or words. Each time, she'd asked about it. And each time, I'd had to brush her off.

Not above taking advantage to dig deep and help her girls, she asked outright, "What is going on with you lately, Randy?"

"Nothing, Mom. I'm all good."

"Nope," she said with a pop. "I heard it before. Now I can see it in your eyes. You're tired and worried."

"Thanks for pointing out my bags," I said sarcastically to deflect, but she was a master. Much like a guard dog on high alert, she went into investigation mode when she sensed something was wrong with one of her daughters.

"Come on. Out with it. Something is bothering you, and you need to talk about it."

"Now, Randy." Dad's slow voice drawled. "If you're having problems, let us know. We can help you."

I waved my hands under the camera so they couldn't see. I needed Merry and Mia to back me up and quick.

"It's nothing bad, promise," I said. "Everything is going well for me, right?" I blatantly looked at my sisters for backup then.

Mia piped up. "Uh, yeah. All great. Warm Regards is blowing up on Insta."

"Yeah," I said. It was true and all, but it was also a lifeline in this conversation. "Business is so good, I'm hiring more café workers and a baking assistant. Takes a lot of time, so I'm working more than usual."

Mom grumbled, obviously still suspicious, but Dad jumped in before she could call me on it. "That's great, hon. So proud of you. Me and your mom knew you'd succeed. You're a fighter."

I swallowed, more touched by his words than he knew. I'd been fighting for weeks, in so many ways. To have my dad confirm it was always a part of me felt good.

"Yep." Mom chimed in, momentarily distracted from her interrogation to sing my praises, another thing she loved to do for her girls. "You were always a big dreamer too." She laughed for a moment and said, "Gosh, when you were little, you used to wake up from your naps and talk about the strangest things."

I stilled, homing in on her words, wanting more information. "Like, what kind of strange things?"

"Oh, you know. Weird places and people. You even did the creepy kid thing where you'd talk about something, and it sounded like you knew stuff you shouldn't have known."

"What?" I wheezed.

Beside me, Merry and Mia froze, waiting to hear more. I'd filled them in on the dream-walking business before we had started this video call.

She laughed, turned to Dad, and said, "Remember when she acted like she already knew I was pregnant with Merry? It was so funny."

He chuckled along with her as she turned back to the camera.

"I was only a few months pregnant. We hadn't even talked to you about it yet because you were so little, and one morning, when you came to wake us up, you asked us when the baby was coming home. We questioned you about it and you were adamant, even pouting about it and demanding it happen right then. You knew a baby was coming home, and you wanted it."

"You did things like that all the time when you were tiny, but it all stopped when..." Dad trailed off. It wasn't like we didn't talk about my powers, but it wasn't something we brought up often, so it could be awkward.

"I stopped having those kinds of dreams when I started being able to go into the shadow world?" I asked outright.

"Around then, yeah. You woke up screaming one night, so scared you wouldn't sleep for two days. We thought something was wrong. You eventually calmed down and slept. Not long after was the first time we noticed you disappearing. Then, well, we all learned about your powers," Mom whispered.

I stared up at the ceiling, my mind racing. How were all these powers connected? Did using my magic more and more make it easier for me to do something I could already do but had blocked out for whatever horrifying reason?

Mia jumped in to fill the silence and give me time to process. "Wow. That's all super interesting. What weird things did I say as a baby?"

Mom and Dad launched into a baby Mia story and everyone laughed at her toddler shenanigans. Everyone but me. I faked it, so they didn't freak out again and worry, but inside I was going over and over my childhood, trying to remember if there was anything else I forgot, anything hinting at dream-walking in my past.

Not long after they had dropped those bombshells, we signed off. As soon as Mom and Dad disconnected, Mia turned to me. "Did you remember any of what they talked about?"

"No," I said.

"Me neither, and I thought we'd heard every childhood story ever from those two," Merry muttered.

"Truth," Mia replied. After thinking for a minute, she said, "Okay. You apparently did the dream-walking before. Now you're doing it again. It scared you as a kid, but it didn't seem to really hurt you. It's a good sign, right?"

"I guess, though it's not great to know I did other magical type things as a kid and just stopped for some reason. Doesn't make a whole lot of sense."

"Does any of this make sense?" Merry asked in her gentle way.

I chuckled. "Nope. I'd like it to, but no, it does not."

She shrugged. "You need to learn more, practice more, and maybe you'll get more answers. You should talk to Harley about this."

"I will, don't worry."

"Speaking of Harley," Mia said, then cleared her throat.

Merry gave a sigh and muttered, "Harley and I went out on a date last night."

"WHAT?" I yelled. "How? Why? Where? Why?"

Mia laughed at my string of ridiculous questions. "The why seems obvious, right?"

Merry continued. "We've been texting..."

I scoffed. "Harley doesn't text. It's all short, curt phone calls or nothing."

"She texts with Merry," Mia singsonged in the loving but grating way only younger sisters could achieve.

"Yes, we text. We have been for a while, since I contacted her to see how I could help."

"You don't need to help."

"I do," Merry said, her voice firm. "Mia does research. You have magic. I can't do those things, but I can do other stuff. I'm not helpless."

"No one said you were," I replied, hating the idea she felt helpless or unneeded, even for a moment.

"Harley gave me some financials to scour for information. It didn't turn up anything useful, but it still felt good to be active in all this. We started talking more, which is where we are now. Talking and going on dates."

"I don't know..."

Merry held up her hand to stop me. "Don't go all big sister on me, Randy. This is why Mia knew before you."

"Unfair. I am your big sister, so I have the privilege of being able to act all big sister-y whenever I want." I paused a moment, then admitted, "I see your point. There's too much other crap going on right now for me to be all snippy about who you choose to date. My concern is all about your safety because I don't want you any deeper in all this magic business. You're already in it though, so maybe it's a pointless worry. I won't tell you not to date Harley, even if I think you should stay far away from mages, because who knows what will happen when they're around? I'll even agree Harley is cool and someone I like and respect."

Merry smiled, big and bright, and said, "Good, because the date went really well."

"Do tell." Mia leaned in, ready for the gossip.

I laughed. "Yeah, sis. Give us the details."

Merry gave a coy smile but told us what amounted to pretty tame details of a first date, which actually sounded nice and sweet. It made me happy for her and, though I hadn't known her long, Harley too. If in all this crazy tumble of magic and mayhem, they could find a special spark, it'd be a good thing.

Twenty

I practiced with Harley and on my own every day for about a week. I was exhausted but came to trust my magic and DD more and more. Came to think about DD and the thrum inside as something I could rely on if need be, and not strictly for major, magical tasks or spells. I discovered I could use the thrum to sense when things in my oven finished baking. Most pro bakers had internal timers, but this was something else, something more precise. It even beat the atomic alarm on my phone. DD was good at mundane tasks like turning on and off light switches. I even started asking it to lock and unlock doors, a very handy trick. DD would whip in, condense down, penetrate the smallest of places, and do its thing.

I practiced with the DD spear too. I watched YouTube videos from martial arts masters and hoped for the best, though this part was slow going. I wasn't used to weapons. Had never needed one before. Now I was trying to twirl a long-ass spear like it was a baton while trying to not smack myself in the face with it. I got bruised and banged up as I became more comfortable with it.

Through all this, the most important aspect seemed to be my comfort level. Magic wasn't only something I had. As Gareth had said, it was a part of me somehow, and each day I worked with it, got used to the thrum's ebbs and flows and the silent, shivering communication of DD, the more comfortable I felt in my own abilities, my own skin. Magic slowly became a small but integrated part of my life, an extension of myself. It felt damn good to know I had power and control. I could do things rather than let things happen to me. I was no longer hiding from myself, and I was starting to love it a little.

When I dreamed again, it went differently because of all my work and self-assurance.

A week to the day of my last dream, during another equally lazy Monday evening of mindless streaming, I fell asleep on the couch and found myself in front of the black church in a toga. This time, I was more curious than afraid. I didn't touch the wood again though. The wound on my finger wasn't fully healed; a dull ache ran all the way to my shoulder. Luckily, same as before, the big wooden doors opened and closed for me without my touch.

I walked, steady though not in a rush, toward the altar, to the door beyond, my thrum telling me where I needed to go. Stepping closer, I studied the chains, wondering if I could get DD to break them apart. When

I went to pick the end up to examine it closer, my hazy hand didn't make contact. It passed through like a ghost. Odd. I tried it on the door, which upon closer inspection I found was not made of the same black wood, but regular wood and iron painted black, to make it blend in with its surroundings, like someone had added this section after they'd originally built the church. Black otherworldly wood, not good. Regular old wood and iron, I could breeze through. I had no idea why and I didn't care as I dreamed. Questions could come at another time. Because I didn't know how long I would dream, I focused on action. Spurred on by my thrum, I slipped through the door to see what was on the other side.

Obviously, it was a staircase. What else would it be if I needed to go up into a steeple, right? It was old, iron, and spiraling, and the stairs were not very wide. Probably weren't even to code, but I doubted evil cults considered building codes much. The staircase stood tightly coiled, its sharp curves winding up into the darkness above, the unknown hovering there. At the sight of the darkness, I shivered with my first hints of fear. I trusted myself and my power enough to find out more, so I pushed through it. Whatever was up there might help us take down the cult, take me and my sisters out of their crosshairs, so I had to try, for Harley and Gareth and Merry and Mia and me.

I climbed, hesitant and a little on edge but moving upward until I reached a large trapdoor in a ceiling, chained in the same way the door to the stairs remained chained. It was the same type of wood, same type of chains, so I pushed through and rose into a small, dingy room. The height, the shape, and the slats letting in minimal amounts of night breeze all told me it was the actual steeple. It was a tiny box lined with crusty old green carpet. A small space with little wiggle room. At least, little wiggle room for the massive beast who was looking me right in my eye.

I froze, feeling like prey. I mean, I'd never felt hunted before, not in a genuine sense. I'd felt danger plenty of times, in this new magical underworld and in the regular old world, but nothing like this. Something older than me, a primal instinct, reared up and made itself known. Tapped me from the lizard part of my brain and told me to freeze, to be afraid of the type of destruction and death that came along with teeth and claws.

The beast looked like a male lion, all big, tight muscle and wide, wild mane. Except this lion was pitch black and about three times the size of any lion I'd seen thanks to Jack Hanna and the Columbus Zoo. He took up about half the small room, filling the rest of the space with his aura or whatever it was called. It was power, big and a lot of it, and the thrum inside me became a steady whine, a long, sharp note. Both made the hair on my arm stand up straight.

Then, I heard the same purr as last time... a shuffling of body and paw as it remained close to the ground until the black lion was staring into my eyes from inches away. They were black pits. Bottomless, yes, but not void or evil or mean. Old NASA images of deep space came to mind: beautiful, dark, and unknowable but with traces of the potential for something more. Those eyes slowed my heartbeat a bit, though I still wasn't too happy with what was in front of me. His tongue shot out to lick his big lion lips, and he stretched his enormous neck out, his nose turned up and twitching as if he scented the air, an ancient-looking cracked leather collar cinched around his throat. Then, an honest-to-God smile. The lion smiled, bent his head, and licked my good hand with its massive, cat-scratchy tongue.

When he moved to sniff the other and I pulled back because of the ache still present after my last dream-walk, he huffed out as if agitated and quickly but gently took my hand in his giant maw. I thought for a moment I was gone; my arm would soon end in a bloody stump, and I'd bleed out in a dreamland. Instead, he sucked my throbbing finger, and a tingle traveled from my finger to my shoulder. In an instant, the lingering pain was gone. Whatever had happened to me, this beast had noticed and healed it.

I was so relieved the ache and tension in my arm was gone, I smiled and scratched the beast on the chin with my other hand as he let the now-healed one slip from his mouth. His purr thundered, filling the room and warming it. He pulled away after a moment, shuffled back against the far wall, and gave a shake of his head, his mighty mane cascading all around like gathered threads of night. "Soon" echoed with the same voice as before, and I knew, without doubt, the beast before me and the man from my vision in the club were the same, and he had no wish to hurt me. Might even help me if I needed it.

"Soon," I whispered back, smiling, and woke again on my couch. This time, I had no injuries. I did, however, have a gross hand covered in beastly lion spittle, so there was that.

DATE TWO WITH GARETH had been uneventful in good and bad ways. No life-threatening events had occurred, which was good. We didn't go beyond a brief make-out session in the back lot after a delicious dinner at one of my favorite Indian restaurants. It was hot, but Gareth pulled back, gave a final quick kiss to my forehead, and sauntered away before I could ask him to come upstairs with me. I was okay with it, because I stayed at a constant level of exhaustion from all the swirling shit, but I would be lying if I didn't add there had been a little disappointment there. Which was why at our last self-defense training session, when we had been practicing frontal attacks and my skin hummed wherever he touched me, I'd asked him to come over for a movie night.

He had agreed, so I was finishing homemade caramel corn when he rang the downstairs bell. I greeted him with a smile and comfy pajamas, though the pajamas I'd chosen may have been a little tight in the shorts area. I knew it was a good call when he met me with a smile, then, a split second later, his gaze locked on the fabric snug and bunched around my round thighs. I made sure to give him a good show of my lovely and ample ass as I led him up the stairs.

He had also dressed for comfort, sporting basketball shorts and a T-shirt, both baggy but clinging in spots so it highlighted the hills and valleys of his large muscles whenever he moved. I may have drooled a little, but I hid it in my love of caramel corn.

We snuggled up on the couch, fluffy blanket thrown over us and various snacks between us, and I pulled up one of my favorite movies.

"This fine with you?" I asked, as the original *Halloween* started rolling.

"Sure. I'd already guessed you were into horror films," he said on a smile.

"How'd you know?"

"The mostly black clothes, the music, the general demeanor..."

"Fair enough," I replied before stuffing a fistful of gooey caramel corn goodness in my mouth and turning back to the TV.

We eventually got closer, the snacks between us moved or eaten. First came the snuggles, about ten minutes into the movie. Then I started stroking his chest where my hand had been resting. His arm circled me, and his hand started rubbing the spot where he gripped my thigh. We moved closer, our hands roaming as our eyes pretended to pay attention to the TV screen.

My love of *Halloween* ran deep, but not that deep. It was maybe thirty minutes into the movie when I flung the blanket aside, and we abandoned all pretense of watching it. I took the time to stop it though. Michael Myers didn't need to see what was about to go down.

Our mouths clashed, heat and need driving our kisses so there was a slight edge of pain. I didn't mind at all. Gareth bit and nipped, but he also licked and soothed after, driving my desire to a maddening degree.

He pulled back and growled, "You okay?"

"More than okay." I panted back at him, reaching for him so we could continue.

He leaned low, kissing down my neck as he said, "I've been thinking of this, of you, of your taste, for weeks now." His hands skimmed my stomach, my thighs, and reached around to knead the upper swell of my ass as I sat in a lust-filled daze.

After several seconds, I replied, "Ditto, big guy."

"Good. Can I fuck you now?" he asked.

"Maybe I want to do the fucking," I said before I launched myself at him. I straddled his lap, pressing myself onto his massive erection so it rubbed me in just the right spot. When a groan wrenched up my throat, Gareth let out a growl of satisfaction and wrapped his arms around me, searing me with another hard and hungry kiss.

I had hoped we'd have other nights like this, other times to explore, but with everything going on, I was afraid we'd once again get interrupted by something or someone. My lust screamed there was no time to waste, so I quickly stood to remove my clothes and grab the condom I'd discreetly placed within arm's reach.

Gareth stared full on for long seconds, and I let him, his devouring gaze the only thing slowing me down. I was sometimes referred to as chubby, chunky, or curvy. Sometimes as fat. I was all those things, and it could make a girl self-conscious in this world. Not because of the facts themselves, but because of the way others treated a person based on those facts. I loved my body, but even the most body-positive person could feel those oily tendrils of self-doubt. The way Gareth stared, though, thrilled me. Didn't hit any red flags at all. Made me feel safe. It wasn't exactly a boost to my confidence. That was an internal thing I had to maintain. It showed an appreciative lust, so I shoved worry aside and stood there for him, reveling in the hungry look etched into his face.

But I wanted to see more too. "Now you," I said, gesturing toward him.

He wasted little time losing his shirt and shorts, and what I saw sitting naked on my couch was glorious. All tight muscle and sleek masculine grace. Lovely. It was almost intimidating. His general size should've been a clue, but seeing him naked firsthand was truly breathtaking, enough to make me pause and consider the physical logistics. I stopped thinking completely when his hand wrapped tightly around his length and he pumped his fist. A deep groan escaped his throat. My mind focused solely on the warm, hard flesh in front of me, and I was more than ready for him.

I straddled him again, lifting while handing him the condom I had opened. Gareth paused, cleared his throat, and with a roughened voice spoke. "Shouldn't we—"

"We should have sex, right here and now, on this couch," I said, stopping whatever objection he had.

He reached down with the condom, skimming my drenched sex with the back of his hand, and I realized he was checking, making sure I was ready for this before he proceeded. It made me sigh and soften toward him more, this kind man who, even in a lust-filled moment, took time to check. I'd been with men who would never, so it was meaningful.

He slipped on the condom, and I lowered myself, slowly letting him fill me inch by exquisite inch. When I fully seated myself, deliciously full of him in fact, we moaned in unison. I noticed some sigils glowed more brightly, like he was using or drawing magic, but I didn't see any extra floating around. It was a question for another time, because in the moment, all I could clearly focus on was the place where we were joined.

"You feel so good," he said in a gravelly tone.

"Same." I gasped as I rose slowly, going nearly to his tip, only to quickly slam back down.

He groaned, his head falling back to lean against the couch as his hands gripped bitingly to my full hips. "Again."

I gave him what he wanted, the slow-up and harsh-down pace so delicious, it quickly became too much to keep up. When Gareth bent his head to take one of my nipples in his mouth, it was over. I was done. So close to exploding, I barely had to reach for it.

I leveraged his shoulders and sped up my pace, taking him again and again until I was on the verge of orgasm. Gareth must have sensed it because he stayed latched on my breast but took over the motion, hammering into me from below, hitting just the right spot deep inside me while also snaking a hand between us to flick my clit.

I exploded. My head flung back, I closed my eyes, and pure sensation washed over me: the drag of him in and out of me, his finger pressed hard on my nub, and his teeth gently biting into my nipple. The whoosh and fall of pure release took over. I saw stars. Maybe not actual stars, but there were definite sparks going on behind my closed eyes. It was so very, very good.

"Shit," Gareth ground out as he finally lifted his head from my breast. He apparently was also close, so I helped, clenching him inside so he started cursing again, lost his rhythm, and shuddered and groaned. His release was far quieter, but it had a silent intensity. His face wrenched up, almost as if in pain. His beautiful mouth twisted, and his eyes clenched tight. Then came the full and utter relaxation of those same muscles. It was a beautiful thing to watch.

After a few minutes of silence punctuated by ragged breaths, I mumbled, "That was fun."

Gareth chuckled, his voice deep and smooth. "Yes, it was."

I climbed off, and my body felt colder as soon as I did. "You want the bathroom first or..."

"You go ahead," he said, and I quickly complied, not wanting to make him wait long. I should've known he'd want me to go first. Always the gentleman, even after some truly hot sex.

Twenty-One

GARETH AND I FELL asleep together curled close in my bed. The next morning, there were gruff hellos, kisses, and touches. It felt easy. Calm. Like I always felt around Gareth. He didn't push or press me; he was good with everything, a mellow gentleman through and through, which was nice. It allowed the stress-relief hormones post sex to linger a long while throughout the day.

It was a good thing too, because my stress skyrocketed later in the afternoon when Mia and Harley burst through the back kitchen doors as I was finishing up frosting a new blueberry lemon chiffon cupcake recipe I planned to try out on my customers the next day.

"Shit's about to go down, Randy," Mia said as she rounded me and swiped a cupcake.

"Take—"

She shushed me. "Take a pic before I eat it. I know." She fussed with the cupcake, situating it on a small paper doily she pulled from a stack. She swiped a leftover lemon wedge I'd planned to use for tea and a few stray blueberries, situated them all, and snapped a pic with her phone. Turning the screen to me for approval, she said, "There. Happy? Jeez."

I motioned for her to go ahead, and she tore into the wrapping, smearing lemon buttercream across her nose as she took a huge bite.

"So sorry to interrupt your banter," Harley called from behind us, "but there is an actual reason we're here."

"Figured you weren't here to swipe cupcakes," I said sarcastically when I looked back. "Actually, why are you two even together?"

"Mia's been doing some investigating on her own," Harley said, and I couldn't miss the bite in her voice, which made me go a little big sister. Not on Harley but on my actual little sister.

"What the hell have you been doing?" I asked, as Mia gulped down more of the cupcake.

"I take full responsibility for this—"

"Oh, I know you will. Whatever crazy scheme you're about to reveal couldn't have come from anyone else, I'm sure."

Harley stood on, silent, her hands in the pockets of her trousers, as per usual. She turned the hard slash of her mouth down in a disapproving frown as she eyed Mia.

"Well, I may have gotten my hands on a fake cell tower configuration from a friend, and this friend and I may have staked out a section of Upper Arlington

I pinpointed based on what all of you had described when talking about the cult spot. I also may have mined a shit ton of skimmed data until I found certain references, followed that with a little SMS and iMessage hacking, and gotten access to a particularly chatty and not-so-smart cultist's text message records over the past few days."

"What?!" I bellowed. Never knew I had a real bellow in me, but in the annals of ridiculous Mia antics, this was by far the most ridiculous and the most dangerous. "Are you out of your ever-loving mind?"

"Apparently," Harley answered.

"You've both done recon there, so don't act like it's too much for me to do the same," Mia countered.

"It is. It totally is. One, Harley and Gareth are highly trained and knowledgeable in the world of the occult. Two, we have magic. It gives the three of us more protection than whatever it was you had."

Mia shrugged. "I brought my gun along. No need to worry."

"Your gun?! When did you get a gun? How long have you had it? When did you even learn to handle a gun?"

"Unimportant," she said a little too flippantly as I continued to seethe.

DD, either equally upset or mad on my behalf, shook in anger in my periphery.

"We can argue all day, or I can tell you both what I learned, which is really important and kind of time-sensitive, so which do you want?"

I was angry and frustrated and scared to death for my sister, but part of me knew the best course forward was getting the cult so she could be safe if they discovered what she'd done. "Tell us. Still, FYI, I'm telling Mom and Dad you have a gun you carry around with you."

"You tell them about my gun, I'll tell them all about this." Stubborn to the core, like all Carters. Damn it. Mutually assured destruction in the form of sister secrets it was. I heaved out an annoyed sigh and circled my hand at her, urging her to tell us what she knew.

"Okay, so I found and tracked messages from someone I'm ninety-nine point nine-nine percent certain is in Starry Wisdom. He made some weird references and mentioned things like magic and something he called 'the black beast' who was supposed to be all-powerful and all-knowing or something."

I thought back to the black lion of my dream, the power there but also the lack of fear I'd had, the help he had given to me in my injury, and the obvious connection between it and the man I had seen projected at Heatwave. Beastly in shape, yes, but maybe not exactly a beast, at least by my definition.

"Interesting," Harley muttered, her forehead creased in thought at the specific references. "Please continue, Mia."

"They're gathering to do something big, and I assume it's something none of us would like too much. It involves pulling power from this black beast, and it's going down Thursday night."

Only three days away. Not a lot of time. I'd felt the power of the black lion in my dreams. If they could siphon this power, it wouldn't be good at all.

"I've seen it, this black beast or whatever."

"Excuse me?" Harley said, her voice like a shard of ice. She turned her deep-brown eyes on me, and I told her everything. She already knew a lot about my dreams, but I hadn't told her the latest version, the one when the black lion had helped me heal from the weird wood splinter. Also meant I had to tell her I hadn't exactly healed from the splinter, which was something I may have omitted when she had asked about the injury before.

Harley bit out a series of curse words and then looked from me to Mia. "You Carter sisters are going to be the death of me. I see it," she muttered.

"Merry's the sweet one, but she has this same stubborn streak. Don't let her fool you," Mia said with fake sweetness.

Harley harrumphed, and I'd never actually heard someone clearly harrumph in conversation before, so it made me chuckle. She didn't appreciate it.

"You both have given me a lot to think over, but we don't have much time. I'm going home to consult a few books and contact my friend who's been studying the wood splinter taken from the dream. I'll be back here in two hours, and we can all talk."

"I'll let Gareth know," I said, and Harley agreed.

"I'll text Merry," Mia said.

"Unnecessary," Harley grumbled. "She doesn't need to come." Part of me was happy Harley felt the need to protect my sister, but I'd known Merry her whole life, and the four of us meeting without her would not fly.

"She's all sweetness until she needs to bite, then she will. For your own benefit, you want her here instead of her finding out about it after the fact," I said, backing up Mia's earlier joking, but still very accurate, assessment. People sometimes wrongly viewed our sister as timid because of her easy outward kindness and quieter nature. "I'm not taking on Merry's wrath, even if you think you are fine with doing it."

Harley sighed and shook her head, heading for the door without another word.

"Okay then," Mia muttered.

I spun on her. "I cannot believe you," I hissed.

"Me? What about you, hanging with demons in your dreams and whatnot."

"He's not a demon," I said, maybe a tad too defensively.

"How would you know?" she asked.

"I'd just know."

Mia snorted a laugh, unbelieving.

"Mia, this is serious. What I can do makes me feel things, sense things, and I know I'm connected to this black lion somehow. Connected enough to know he's powerful and dangerous in his own way but not a threat to me or humanity at large somehow. I can't explain it, but I KNOW. It's here," I said, patting my chest and referencing the thrum of magic I constantly felt resonating.

Her eyes softened, and she pulled me in to a hug, revealing the tension in her petite body. "I did it for you, Randy. Because you needed the help, needed to know," she muttered, the side of her face lying against my shoulder in the way she always had, even when she had been a baby, burrowing there deep and cozy to find comfort.

I closed my eyes, fear and stress racing through me, but I understood. As I held my sister, I couldn't help but understand what it meant to want to help someone you loved with every part of yourself. "I know. I also know you can take care of yourself, apparently in ways I didn't even realize, Little Miss Annie Oakley, but this world we're in now is the same but also different, and the danger is different. We adjust and remember, learn to be a little more cautious, right?"

She bobbed her head, a moving weight on my shoulder. A good weight. I held on tight, and we both separated, only to get to work on whatever might help us, help Harley, and help Columbus. Maybe even help the world.

HARLEY SHOWED UP EXACTLY two hours later with Merry, fuming, by her side. Merry then proceeded to rip into me, Mia, and Harley as we stood like chastised schoolchildren in front of her. Her tirade lasted long enough Gareth caught the tail end of it when he slipped into the kitchen.

"Never again. You hear me? Never again. This commando 'I do it on my own and leave poor Merry in the dark' is done. Am I heard?"

Mia and I agreed. Harley had a smirk on her face, like she enjoyed being told off or something, and said in a too-husky voice, "Heard."

Merry, still fuming, sniffed and spun on her heals, arms crossed on her chest, and gave Gareth a hard look up and down. "You. Did you know anything about all this?"

"I'm sorry, Meredith, but I don't exactly know what all this is," he admitted.

She told him, then he was upset, though it was a quiet upset he didn't voice. I could see it though, in the hard stance in his body and the deep frown on his usually smiling face.

"As we're all now properly told off and up to date," Harley said, "let's talk about what we need to do next." She took her hand from her pocket and pulled out a small notebook, bound in red leather, and consulted some notes.

"This is what we know. Starry Wisdom is planning some ritual, likely a siphon or transference ritual, which would allow them to draw immense power from the black lion Randy's interacted with in her dreams.

The dreams, in fact, may have been a warning about this, the reason she was dreaming of the black lion to begin with. Regardless, it would not be good if Starry Wisdom taps into more power. They need to be stopped and stopped permanently, if possible."

"But how?" I blurted.

"I have a plan. My friend, the one who studied the sliver of wood, believes it to be seeped in some form of interdimensional magic, which allows it to be on our world but flit between worlds if necessary. The magic is dark, which is why it slithered into Randy and hurt her even after she took the splinter out. He found a spell, very old and very strong. It could strip the power away. The casting is tricky and will take time to pull off, but if we leech out the magic from the wood itself, it could become vulnerable to something like Crumbling Flame."

"A spell I know well," Gareth said.

Harley gave him a chin lift in acknowledgment and continued. "The cult loses a huge power source if we take out the magic seeped into the wood of the building. We stop the transference, or siphon, too, and it all crashes down. No more well of power to draw on, no more Starry Wisdom—or no more Starry Wisdom with all the power of the black church at their disposal. Makes them much easier to stop in a more permanent way."

"That's it? Take out the building, and Starry Wisdom goes poof?" I asked, mimicking an explosion with my upturned hand.

"Maybe not completely or instantaneously," Harley answered, "but mostly, I think so."

She paused a second to let the idea sink in before she went on. "Which brings me to the plan. Thursday, Gareth, Randy, and I get to the area early, sneak on the grounds, and wait for signs the ritual is about to begin. When they're distracted, we do a quick blitz attack to force the bulk to scatter. Randy shields me as I set up and perform the spell, which will take a lot of time and energy. Gareth and Randy hold any stragglers off long enough to get me through it, then Gareth sets off Crumbling Flame. Starry Wisdom, at least as we know it, is then no more."

"The people, the cultists? What happens to them?" I asked, needing to voice it. We were talking about battle, even if it was a magical battle. Were we actually going to kill people?

Harley eyed me, then said in a low voice, "You know this has to be done. And at least some of the cult will not back down, will not yield."

I sighed, knowing what she meant. She was right, of course. I'd asked for this when I'd pressed for an attack after Macy had shown up in the café. I hadn't acknowledged what it meant, but deep down I knew, and in my anger, I'd wanted it. Calmed now, I didn't like it, yet I also recognized it was necessary.

Mia and Merry hugged me on each side, and Merry said with vehemence, "You do what you need to do to come back to us. Those people made their choices. They hurt and killed others or stood by while others in their ranks did the dirty work. So you do whatever you have to do to get back here to us."

I nodded, though I didn't know if I could do it, or even what it might mean about who I was as a person if I could.

"I get it, I do. To pull it off though, I need you two," I said, looking back and forth from sister to sister, "to keep yourself safe and far away."

"But—" Mia began as Merry made an annoyed sound before I stopped them both short.

"I need to know you're safe. I can't do what may need to be done if I'm worried about you. The best way you can help me, help all of us, is to lie low and stay safe. In fact, I'd like you to stay here and wait for us. I'll add some wards I've learned to what Gareth put up."

Harley stepped up then. "I'll add my own as well. We'll make Warm Regards nearly impenetrable."

Merry looked around at us, her sister, and the woman she was dating, and said, "Okay."

Mia protested again, and I grabbed her hands. "Please, Mia. I need this," I pleaded.

"I need to help," she whispered. "I don't like you going out there alone."

"I'm not," I said on a sad smile. "I've got Harley and Gareth. You'll have Merry. You can look after each other. Keep each other safe."

"I want to keep us all safe," she said.

"I know. So do I. Which is why I need you to promise me you'll stay out of this fight."

She heaved a deep breath in, closed her eyes, and nodded. When she looked at me, there were tears there. "This is serious shit, and I don't like you doing serious shit without me behind you."

"You are. You did your part, and you did it so well. Let us do ours without having to worry."

We hugged, the Carter sisters a small cluster of near tears and worry and fear in my shiny kitchen. Gareth gave us space, as did Harley. They went out to throw up stronger wards, as I'd do soon enough. First, I needed to hold my sisters close, if only for a moment, before I moved on to magic.

Twenty-Two

WE HAD THREE DAYS. Two, actually, since Mia got the info and we'd made our plan on a Monday. It left Tuesday and Wednesday for prep because Thursday was the big show. We already had a schedule in place we could revamp to give us more time to work together.

The big issues for us were timing, spellwork, and intention. Harley, Gareth, and I needed at least some practice performing magic together. It helped we'd worked together as a unit some during my training. Besides, each of us was used to the others. We'd never done magics as a trio, and what we needed to do required timing and work while doing our own thing individually. Teamwork made the dream work and all that, so practice was necessary.

Spellwork was also important, especially for Harley, who would be doing a wicked-hard spell she'd never performed before and couldn't exactly practice. It was a spell of interdimensional untethering. We didn't want to accidentally untether any old real-world object, hence no practice. She could work through some steps, memorize things, and so on, but she'd have to do it all together for the first time when we needed it to work the most. I didn't envy her the pressure, though she bore it well, and I knew, in my mind and my gut, she had what it took to pull it off.

Gareth practiced the Crumbling Flame spell a little, but he'd had it down before. No idea why he needed or wanted to learn a magical spell of utter destruction, but it came in clutch in this moment, so I wouldn't ask. With Harley to contain it, he manifested the force a few times to make sure he still had it and there were no hiccups, so his end was sound.

Both Gareth and I practiced defensive and offensive magic. I knew a handful and didn't trust anything new, so I focused solely on those, in Harley's gym and my makeshift practice space next to my apartment. I also spent a lot of time meditating, connecting with my thrum of magic and communicating mentally with DD. We didn't need either of them, as new as they were, breaking down in the middle of some magical brawl.

Gareth took a few days off from the library, telling them he had an emergency pop up. I let Deb take over Warm Regards, baking as much stock as I could between practice sessions with Harley and Gareth. I spent time alone working my spear, practicing thrusts and throws just in case. Oddly, I daydreamed about how easy this all could be if I got around to hiring a baking assistant, but I stopped thinking about it real quick. One, I didn't want this to be my life forever. I wanted to stop the cult and go back to worrying only about the baking. Two, who even knew if I'd make it past Thursday?

That final thought brought me to Harley's place early on Wednesday afternoon. We'd decided on one final practice session together before we peeled off and went our separate ways for the night, Harley to chat with her friend who'd given her the rundown on the wood and me and Gareth to do some extra physical fight training at their gym. He insisted I do more last-minute physical training. Plus, he wanted to see me work with my spear, try to help me practice physically fighting with my magical-but-still-very-physical weapon if he could.

"You're early, and I have things to do," Harley said after she opened the door to me and immediately turned around to walk away.

I followed her in and down, into the office and practice space. She had books on books on books, all opened to various pages. Papers lay strewn about. It was a study tornado.

"How's all this going?" I asked, gesturing toward the stacks of research.

"As good as I could expect with little notice. I hope it's enough," she answered in an offhanded manner, distracted by everything she was thinking, planning, and doing.

"Yeah. About that..." I trailed off, not wanting to voice what I needed to voice but still needing to say it.

Harley turned, her arms crossed and her expression serious. She stood silently, not in judgment but to let me continue at my own pace. "If—not that it will—but if something were to happen tomorrow—happen to me, I mean—I'd like you to promise me something."

Her face, so often stoic, softened a touch. "Randy, I..."

"No, Harley. I don't want you to lie. You've never done it before. You've always been honest with me, and I appreciate it. I also don't want to hear your honesty right now because I know. Even if I don't have too much experience in this occult world, I know what we're about to do is dangerous. Life-and-death dangerous." I paused, took a few breaths to calm my nerves, and continued.

"I want you to promise me you'll make sure Merry and Mia, and my parents, are safe. That they stay safe, as best you can. Wards, sigils, whatever magic it takes, I don't want them to suffer because of what I am and what we're about to do."

"Of course. I promise, I will make sure the entire Carter family remains safe and protected if something were to happen."

"Thanks. I know you will, and you can, so I appreciate you agreeing."

She didn't act like it wasn't a big deal. We both knew everything connected to what we were about to do was a big deal. She did, however, clear her throat and say, "If something were to happen to me, I'd ask you to tell

Merry I'm sorry. Sorry that, in all my decades of time, I didn't have enough to get to know her more."

Instant tears welled in my eyes. I gave a watery smile. Not pressing either of them on their relationship had been the right call. Not only because it wasn't my place but because of this, the evidence of something beautiful already growing between them. I wanted beauty and happiness and a bright future for them both, so I echoed Harley's words back to her. "Of course."

I cleared my throat, trying to dislodge the sob stuck there as Harley strode away, back to her books with her head down, possibly trying to hide her own emotions. I didn't need to pry, so I let her have her space. "I have more to read before our training," she called back to me.

"Yep. I'll be over here, practicing with DD. Do what you have to do. I'm cool."

She sat in her reading chair, flipping through books and shuffling loose papers, while I stood at the opposite end of the vast room, DD zipping around as I thought. I'd gotten better at dividing it and doing multiple things at once, but controlling everything at the same time was tricky.

The two of us did our own thing as we waited for Gareth to show, apart but a part of something together, in this magic and now in the usual yet no less special way all humans had of creating connections through time with care, concern, and growing love in all its beautiful variations.

WHEN I MET UP for my solo time with Gareth later that night, the gym didn't have its usual sounds. No big men beating each other or pounding on bags. The main lights were off, leaving only the soft glow of the occasional utilitarian sconces scattered along the walls and the small but bright hallway light. It was always slightly eerie to enter a place usually filled with activity and find it empty, and this felt like it, like a place pulled out of time.

Maybe my morose mood was shading it, but whatever. Gareth was a highlight, waiting for me with a tight smile. His smile had been tight for the last few days, likely with the same types of thoughts and worries I'd discussed with Harley.

"Let's get our fight on," I said, forcing a chipper tone to help ease some of the heaviness of the room, the space between us.

"First, let me see the spear."

Gareth hadn't seen it before then. I had no problem showing him, so I shrugged and manifested the spear, the pitch black of it making it nearly invisible in the dull lighting of the gym, a solid shadow I somehow could puff in and out of existence at will.

"Show me what you can do," Gareth said after studying the spear in my hand for a few minutes.

It wasn't much, but I showed him my twirl, my thrusts, my throws. He helped me strengthen my stances, my grip, and my sense of targeting.

We spent maybe thirty minutes on it before I asked, "Good?"

He kept the tight smile he'd had plastered on his face all night and nodded, handing me the small sparring gloves we often used without a word as I blinked the spear back into DD's quivering ball. Our training continued with little talk and was demanding, Gareth giving clipped instructions the whole time.

He focused on hits and kicks, with a few blocks thrown in for good measure. It was an offensive lesson, and I couldn't help but think he did it because he knew I'd have to fight someone tomorrow night and he wanted me prepared.

After a grueling forty-five minutes of nonstop punches, kicks, and blocks, I called time. My arms and legs were noodles, and I needed a break. I took a long pull from my water bottle and sat, catching my breath on the bench along the wall, my elbows to my knees, my eyes on the ground a few feet in front of me. Gareth eventually sat beside me, his body a warmth against my side. He didn't speak, and as we sat there, I felt something else creep over him. Not exactly something else, more like a slight absence of something. Then the realization hit me, and my worry about Gareth ratcheted up a notch. Tonight, he'd exuded far less of that calming presence I experienced when I hung out with him. It was there, faintly, but not at all like what I normally felt around the big guy. He'd kept his distance as he'd instructed me. Having him close made me mark the change.

He'd been too quiet at Harley's and was silent now, so I needed to step into his silence. "You okay?" I asked, cocking my head in his direction.

"Not exactly," he grumbled.

"Fair enough. Don't think any of us are okay at the moment. I guess what I mean is do you want to talk about it? You don't have to. If you do, I'm here."

He slumped back, his head tilted upward to stare at the ceiling as he talked. "I'm worried. We're all worried, I know, but I'm specifically worried about you." He slid his eyes toward mine as he slid his hand to my leg and gave it a squeeze. "I don't want to see you hurt."

"I don't want to see me hurt either." I laughed, trying to lighten the mood with no success. "For real, I don't want to see you hurt either. I don't want any of us getting hurt. On a broader level, I don't want anyone to be hurt by Starry Wisdom. That's why we've got to do what we're going to do tomorrow."

"All this is new to you, magic and fighting. I wish you didn't have to get into it so soon."

"Same, but we don't always get what we want in life. We handle what we get and hope for the best."

"Wise advice, even if it is hard to accept." He leaned close then, moving his hand from my leg to rub across my cheek.

I leaned into it, enjoying the feel of him on my skin, the touch causing my core to clench.

"I just want you to know I think you're amazing, Randy."

"You're pretty amazing yourself, big guy." I smiled at him, bright and true, because he was amazing. Kind and smart and thoughtful. I cared for him deeply, even though we'd known each other only for a brief time. A season. He had lodged himself in my heart firmly. It wasn't an all-consuming romantic love, but it was care and love that mattered nonetheless.

I turned my head slightly to kiss the inside of his palm and watched as his eyes flared, changing from worried to heated in a blink. He grabbed my cheeks and moved me, maneuvering us both so our lips met in the middle. It was a soft, almost reverent kiss at first, a moment to acknowledge the sweetness in what we seemed to have. It turned hungrier, harder, soon enough.

We sat on the bench, clutching each other, our lips clashing, until Gareth pulled away to grab the hem of my shirt and rip it over my head. He growled in frustration at my sports bra. Those things were hard to get out of in a hurry. I laughed and helped him wiggle it up and over my head. I sat, my breasts free and my nipples turning hard because of the cool gym air and Gareth's stare. He sat still, staring at my chest, before he moved his head toward mine, leaned into me forehead-to-forehead, and took a long breath.

"Are you okay with this?" he asked. I knew if I wasn't, he'd stop immediately. He'd stopped to ask, reeled himself in to make sure I was okay. It was who he was, and it made me soften a bit.

"Yes. Please. Yes," I called, pulling him forward, giving him another hungry, pleading kiss. I needed the release and relief, but more. I also needed connection and feeling. Gareth gave me both.

Soon, his shirt was off, then my leggings and panties were next. He stood me up to strip them down, trailing heated kisses from my thighs to my feet as he removed them inch by torturous inch. Gareth stayed on his knees a moment, looking up at me with such lust in his eyes, it made me a little woozy to see.

He placed a soft kiss to my mound, his tongue a whisper along my seam. Just enough to make me shiver and want more, but he didn't give it. He instead grabbed a condom from his open gym bag and moved me to a blank section of wall a few steps away, spinning me quickly so the cool stone pushed against my front. His warm body leaned over me, pressing me, as he whispered, "Are you fine with quick and hard? I wanted to give you more time and attention, but I don't think..."

He trailed off, and I filled in the silence. "Quick and hard is more than fine, Gareth."

A rumble sounded from his chest, and he took the time to push his pants and boxers down enough to pull himself free. He tested my wetness with his fingers, and I groaned at the soft touch. Then, a slight nudge of his feet widened my stance, and his hard length nudged deeper, homing in on my entrance a second before he slammed home.

It was hard, like he'd said. The concrete did delicious things to my nipples as he pushed my body again and again to the wall, a dulled scrape heightening my sensitivity. The sound of slick flesh on flesh slapped in the silent space, the quiet punctuated by our panting breaths. We didn't say anything. Didn't need to. We needed to get lost in something that felt magical but wasn't the magic shitstorm rolling around us.

Gareth's hands at my hips dug in, a small bite of pain I appreciated. He kept a relentless pace, slamming in and pulling out quickly, snapping his hips in a rough beat, hitting something deep inside so packed with tingling sensation I began to whimper. When he heard it, he snaked one arm around and pressed it between my body and the wall to find my clit and rub it furiously.

"Come for me," he bit out, and in moments, I did, screaming my release. He rode me through it, pounding harder, somehow even deeper, until his beat became erratic. He shuddered, let out his own strained curse, and ground into me as he twitched in release inside me.

We stood there catching our breath for a good minute. Eventually he pulled out, moving my slightly damp hair aside to give me a kiss on my upper back.

"Be right back," he muttered, moving to the restroom in the hallway.

I quickly dressed and did the same, and when I came out, I found him seated at the wall bench again, a softer smile on his face.

"Hey," he said, his voice rougher than normal.

"Hey," I said back, my voice smoother and brighter than it was earlier. Taking my seat beside him, sitting close, I said, "Again. Fun," and he laughed, a deep belly laugh I was happy to hear.

"Yes. Fun."

"Also stress-relieving, so thanks."

"No need to thank me for sex. Ever." He chuckled to himself before turning to give me a sweet, almost chaste kiss on the mouth. "Are you fine?"

"Completely. Though I need to at least attempt to get some sleep tonight. Think I might even do it, what with your punishing training and hot sex."

He smiled. "A pleasure to serve."

We packed up and said quick good-byes. He stayed back to lock up the gym, and I made my way home, back to Warm Regards in hopes of sleep and maybe even a good, informative dream where I might find a little extra help.

HARLEY AND GARETH PICKED me up at Warm Regards around four the following afternoon. My stomach had churned all day, dread creeping in for what was going to go down. I wasn't a soldier, hardened to battle. I was a baker. I'd been in a total of one slap fight with another girl when I was thirteen after she'd called Merry a derogatory name. I had no experience, no frame of reference, for what was to come, and I wished with everything I had it didn't have to be this way.

It was, and I had to go. To pull out would leave Harley and Gareth unprotected, my sisters and parents unprotected, Columbus—and even possibly the whole wide world—unprotected. I couldn't have that, even if I felt like I was going to hurl up the minimal amount of food I'd forced down my throat.

We rode in Harley's car, a black luxury sedan which, somehow, looked stylish and nondescript at the same time. Perfect for Harley, really. I got a chin lift from Harley via the rearview mirror when I scooted into the back seat. Gareth turned and offered me the tight smile he had last night. Seems the sex afterglow only lasted so long when life and death were hanging in the balance. Couldn't fault him though. I'd been nice and relaxed when I'd shuffled into my apartment, but the nerves had creeped back in by the time I was in bed, and they'd raged higher and hotter ever since. I simply offered my own forced smile and no words to either. No words came from anyone. We spent the quick trip to Upper Arlington in silence, each of us locked in our own thoughts.

For my part, I was breathing deep, trying to stay tethered to the magical thrum in my gut and DD at my side. DD was oddly still, though tense like it was ready to snap in a moment. It was a feeling I could relate to, so I sent as much comfort and commiseration down our odd little connection as I could.

We parked several blocks away, deep in an immaculately landscaped neighborhood filled with sprawling ranches and towering mini mansions. For not the first time, I wondered about the place, the oddity of an evil cult hiding in a rich part of Columbus. As I thought on it, it seemed fitting. No one asked residents here questions; no one asked people in any area like this questions. Sinister doings weren't expected in such places, though there were all kinds of evils lurking in grand neighborhoods.

Harley and Gareth went straight to the area where they had set up last time, the night they had met me. It seemed like a lifetime ago, though it was only several weeks past. Enough to change my entire life. All of us nodded, pointed, grunted, or shifted to communicate. We still hadn't broken our silence, and we wouldn't dream of it here, so close to the shelter house downhill from the black church.

At dusk, cultists arrived. We moved up then, toward to the entrance, though keeping quiet and low to avoid detection. Harley used binoculars to keep a close eye on the group while Gareth squatted, stoic and at least outwardly calm. I, however, jumped at the sound of leaves blowing in the breeze and birds landing in branches. I was nervous. Beyond nervous. Terrified.

Harley indicated about fifty people were inside the church when those big black doors creaked closed. They were about to do whatever it was they'd planned to do, so we needed to move. Harley and Gareth remained close to the ground but moved with speed toward the looming church. I followed as best I could, though I wasn't nearly as coordinated, and I stumbled some.

At the doors, two burly men in robes stood guard. Gareth muttered something. A small part of his forearm tattoo glowed, and it was like the guards froze in place. Gareth walked right up to them and pulled a heavy-looking and weirdly shiny gun from his waistband, then hit each in the head with the butt. They fell like sacks of flour, crumpling to the stairs, their tiny trickles of blood barely visible in the moonlight.

I didn't think they were dead, but I wasn't certain and wasn't about to stop to check.

"A gun?" I mouthed and got a shrug in response. Whatever would help, magical or non-magical, was a good thing, I guess.

Harley was at the door, skimming a hand about an inch from the surface, checking the wards and spells there to see how we might enter. I walked up behind her, close so I could listen if she whispered some type of instructions, and there was a barely audible swoosh sound. The doors didn't fling themselves open, but they opened. Much like they had in my dreams. Harley looked back, cocked an eyebrow my way, and it was my turn to shrug. I had no answers, and a convo about exploring random weird things my powers did could wait, since we were about to burst in on a group of evil cult members performing some wicked ritual.

Harley placed one hand on the door, motioned for Gareth to shore up behind us, and indicated I needed to push as well. I touched the door, felt the flow and burn of its wrongness, its magic, and wanted to pull away, but I didn't. Didn't really need to anyway, because with her other hand, Harley counted down from three, and we heaved inside as a unit.

The first few moments were a complete blur. Surprise and adrenaline were on our side. As soon as we entered, the chanting of some incantation remained steady but began to falter. I took in the scene: Macy stood at the altar, her lighter robes stark against the darkness of the church, and her pretty face glowing from nearby candlelight and the surrounding sigils. A few members flanked her on either side, but the bulk of the nameless, faceless cult members stood facing her, their hands and voices raised in incantation and their own sigils glowing with power.

The scene lasted only a split second before Macy let out a frustrated scream and pointed at us, her body visibly shaking—though I couldn't tell if it was anger or a need to unleash some sort of power they'd been trying to manifest. She spoke no words, only pointed, and the cult turned together, their hands falling to their sides, to sneer and growl at us. They sounded like animals ready to hunt, and we were their prey.

They charged, a mob of people bent on hurting us, but we'd known it would happen, so we'd prepared for it. Gareth hit the front with whatever freeze spell he'd had literally up his sleeve and caused a scramble for a moment, as cultists crashed into each other. It didn't stop them. They didn't help their fellow Starry Wisdom followers either. They trampled over each other instead, mindlessly coming our way despite the horrible sounds of boots meeting flesh, sharp cries, and cracking bones.

We moved as one, the three of us needing to be at least a little farther into the space because Harley's spell needed room to work right, which forced us into the narrow aisle between the stiff-backed pews. It was hard, stepping forward when a mob was running toward me, even if it was only a few small steps. Harley dipped down behind me and Gareth to draw a circle of power and sigils on the floor, a necessary setup for the complex spellwork she was about to perform.

Gareth's spell gave us a few seconds of time, but it was enough for me to focus in, call on DD, and do my thing. Instantly, it blanketed the three of us in protection before ballooning outward, creating a bubble that pushed pews aside, then flung people back. They kept coming mindlessly, bouncing off the DD bubble, knocking themselves out in the process when they careened off the shield and hit the ground with a good deal of force. I flinched, watching people injure themselves without thought, without care, simply trying and failing to get what they wanted.

An odd thing happened after those first hectic minutes. As cultists woke up from their frozen or sprawling positions, they didn't redouble their efforts. They took in the scene and ran. People started streaming around the edges of DD, running for the doors. It wasn't everyone, and I wasn't sure why they were doing it, whether they'd been spelled or simply thought the fight wasn't worth it after being knocked unconscious, but it was enough to make a difference.

Those left, however, were the fervent. The top people. The cultists who were die-hard. They also used magic, hitting DD with spells. I didn't know what they would do to the three of us inside the bubble, but DD recoiled as if hurt. It kept up the protection despite the blows.

"Don't know how much of this DD can take," I yelled to Gareth, finally breaking our hours of silence.

He looked back, and I followed his gaze. Harley had finished the circle of power and was sitting crossed-legged within its confines, muttering the incantation in a whisper-soft voice.

"She needs more time to get her own defenses up, but not much," Gareth answered. "Can you hold?"

I nodded and gritted down, sending all my help and hope and intention and care over to DD, wanting to keep it strong but also safe and whole. With each spell, it wavered slightly, but it never broke. I could feel its answering resolve rebound back at me, making my magic thrum on a higher frequency, giving me more determination and confidence.

In our little protective shadow, a soft glow pulsed. I turned to look at Harley and saw the circle she drew on the floor rise, as if floating on rippling water. It didn't break or wash away, simply floated up to about chest height on Harley—a soft white glow of power I could feel pulsing through the area.

Harley, her eyes squinting through the gathering light surrounding her, yelled, "Drop it and move!"

I didn't hesitate. I brought DD back and dove behind a pew, hitting the ground hard enough my teeth chattered in my head. Whatever power raised from the circle flashed out toward the remaining cultists, who screamed. The ones closest to Harley fell to the ground, singed and unmoving. They were toast, literally, and the smell of their burned flesh made my nostrils flex and my stomach heave. The others scattered, running to save themselves in the face of Harley's glowing and lethal magic.

They had nothing to match it, so I didn't blame them. I watched in awe as Harley unfurled from the floor, the circle of power a wave suspended in the air, shimmering around her as both protection and defense. Her voice didn't waver. It didn't break. She called her incantation down without hesitation, with clear will and immense skill. I was new to magic, and even to me, it was amazing to see. For anyone not in our little trio, it was likely terrifying.

As Harley moved toward the center of the space to complete her spell, a spell she warned us would take not only effort but also time, I felt power rise to meet her. I shivered as it crept across my skin. Harley was impenetrable, but I wasn't, and neither was Gareth.

Before I could blink, much less get DD to cover us, I watched from across the aisle as Gareth reared up to send some spell at the power in front of us, then buckled from an invisible blow. His body folded in half as if he'd taken a punch to the gut, and blood flowed from his nose. I screamed and slithered toward him, skimming on my knees to where he lay between two pews across the center aisle.

His hand was up, wiping the blood away as he wheezed breath in and out. "Shield," he croaked, reaching up to stroke my cheek with his bloody fingers, leaving a wet trail on my flesh. I pulled DD over us, protecting us, as I bent toward him.

"It's okay. You're going to be okay." I didn't know if it was true, but he needed it to be. I needed it to be.

"Harley may still need your help. Go," he croaked.

I shook my head, not wanting to leave him, tears falling freely down my face.

"You have to, Randy. Now go."

Damn it. I hated it, but he was right. I couldn't really help him unless we got through this, so I gave his hand a squeeze before rising. I called on DD, asked it to split, creating a protective cocoon around Gareth as it also wafted over me, shielding me as I rose to face the power still trying to penetrate Harley's defenses.

It was Macy. She stood alone at the altar, various sigils on her robes, and her arms flaring as she flung spell after spell right at Harley. She paused when she saw me rise and gave a tinkling laugh.

"Thought you were going to hide this whole time, sugar," she purred before flinging some spell my way. It cracked and withered on DD, though the hit was enough to make the shield weaken in the spot she'd hit. DD couldn't take to much more, and I couldn't have it failing on Gareth, or failing Harley if Macy could somehow get through whatever magic was flowing around her. It was time to fight, not defend.

Twenty-Four

THE SLICING SMIRK ON her lips slipped away when my spear, long and dark and sharp, appeared in my hands.

Fazed for only a second, she cocked her head and said, "Seems you've learned more tricks."

"More than you know," I said, my voice cool even though I was anything but. I was a riot of emotions. Terror was way up there, but anger dominated. Anger at what she'd done to Gareth, to countless others. Anger at her threat to me and mine. It was too much.

"I can show you more, you know. You're capable of so much more." She cooed as if she could entice me after all she'd said and done.

"No, thanks. I don't like to hang with evil murderers. Bad for the karma, you know." I gave a hard, sickly-sweet smile, which Macy returned.

"Too bad. For us, but mostly for you, honey." She didn't continue her pitch but glowed, charging up a spell. Too bad for her, because I didn't need the charge or transfer time. My magic flowed in and through me at my will. I trusted in it now, and before whatever she had pulled up could make its way toward me, I shoved all of my intention into getting to her.

Shadows fell. Not DD, but regular old shadows, though they were dark enough to obscure her vision of me so I could crouch and move, running toward her through the darkness.

She did something that allowed her to see, to glow with a faint red light all around her. She wasn't expecting me to be so close, so she backed up a step when I popped up on her left side. Stumbled before regaining her footing and throwing whatever magic she had called up at me. I didn't have time to shield, though I was lucky enough to dodge the bulk of the force. It cut my flesh like a knife, a sharp point of magic opening a gash across the top of my shoulder, inches from my throat.

Macy had decided she no longer wanted to play. I agreed. I pulled the darkness around me like smoke, swirling it in a dense fog even her red glow couldn't penetrate, and I changed direction, shifting behind her and landing a hard punch to her ribs. She grunted in pain but stayed standing and started flinging magic around, making chunks of black wood explode from the back wall as her spells landed.

They missed me because in the shadows I'd tilted to one side again. I grabbed her with one hand, turning her my way in the hope she'd lose her balance. She was good though, trained, because as she twirled around, she landed a closed-fist blow to my temple even though I was still in the swirl of darkness. It left my head fuzzy for a moment, enough for her to land another punch to my gut and cause my focus to slip enough my shadows dropped, leaving me exposed. I bent over and wheezed. It would've been a great opportunity for her to land more serious blows, with fists or legs or magic, but she made the mistake of reaching for my spear instead. DD didn't take kindly to that, and where her hand tried to grasp it, spiny points grew and pierced through her hand.

Macy screamed, blood pouring down her arm, the red glow surrounding her dimming slightly. It gave me time to right myself and land my blow, a quick kick to the knee, causing her leg to buckle. I slashed out with the staff of the spear, hitting the same leg again.

Macy hit the black wooden floor, and she looked up at me with pure hate in her eyes. "You bitch," she hissed. The sigils on her robes flickered like flames, convulsing as if trying to force through something. Whatever she had in mind was big, but I didn't care. She'd lost focus while I'd sharpened mine.

I brought the spear down, but she rolled away, causing me to drive the tip of the spear into the black floor. The spear was stuck, and as I tried to pull it free, she landed a swift and powerful kick to my ribs.

I went sliding across the floor, my spear finally freed, though it did little good as I curled in around what felt like broken ribs. She stalked forward and sneered down at me, her sweet-sounding voice turning to a near growl of wild hate.

"We could have used your power, but now I think I'll just kill you. Then kill your friends here. Maybe even go find your pretty little sisters and peel parts of them away to see if there's any magic buried deep. I doubt there is, but the process of uncovering a person can be invigorating."

She reared back, pulling power from some siphon or source I couldn't see. It had to be enough for a big spell, given the time it took to gather. But it also gave me enough time to call on DD to shield me before it hit. There was a bang, a crack, and something like the echo of a whimper deep in my mind that made tears fill my eyes. I pushed DD away after the hit, needing to save it, not wanting it to take any more damage.

Macy screamed in frustration and rage, then bent down deep to gather more magic to herself from the black floor, but I was done. Filled with rage at what she'd done and what she said she would do, no longer caring about broken bones or pain, I rushed up and tackled her to the floor. Scrambling on top, I punched her two times in the face, hearing her head snap back and hit the floor, hearing her nose crack.

I didn't hesitate or balk. I called enough DD back to me to cast my weapon, twirled the spear of DD around, grabbed her by the robe, and shoved the tip deep into her left shoulder. She screamed in pain, but it lost steam in the split second it took for me to transport her into the shadow world.

I hadn't known I could do it, but Harley had done it to me, so I figured I'd try it. It worked. We both lay in the shadow world, bleeding from our shoulders, though her wound was worse. Blood covered her once-pristine robes from shoulder to stomach, the faintly glowing sigils barely visible.

I wrenched the spear free, flung it hard to help get the gross cult-leader blood off it, and stood to lean against the long spear, using it as a makeshift crutch to help ease some of my rib pain. I watched as Macy writhed and screamed, then turned more and more quiet and still, once she finally realized where she was.

There wasn't a lot of visual difference between the inside of the black church and the shadow world because of all the black, but a slight gray tinge in the air helped distinguish it. Interestingly, Macy seemed to hear the monsters here too, because the first waves of fear skittered across her ivory face when they became audible in the too-near distance. The sound of slithering things with teeth and mouths and hunger populating this dimension was hard to forget, and Macy must have somehow heard them before, because she was terrified. She showed it in the frantic twist of her pretty face.

"They come quickly for fear. I've seen it myself," I said, her eyes frantic as she searched the area for the direction of the sounds. "Figured blood might also do the trick. Seems I was right."

Macy scrambled to her knees as best she could, trying to stand. She didn't have much luck.

I crouched to look her level in the eye, navy blue to ice blue. "Sounds like they're coming quicker. On one level, not great for you. On another, maybe it will be over soon."

Realization hit her face, and she panicked. "Please," she rasped. "You can't leave me here." She grabbed for my legs, but I kicked out at her wounded shoulder, and she recoiled in pain as she fell back to the floor.

"Can and will."

"I can get out of this. I can get out of this," she said, almost like a chant, before cutting her hate-filled eyes my way. "And when I do, I'll watch everything you love bleed and suffer at my hands."

"Nice threat, lady, but you have to actually back it up. Bye now." I gave a jaunty wave and winked back into my reality, the echo of her scream of hate and fear lingering in my ears as I looked around me.

I didn't have time to think about what I'd done. To help Harley, I had to get rid of Macy. To save Gareth. To make sure Merry and Mia stayed safe. To avert whatever evil scheme she'd come up with next. Didn't mean I wanted to make someone bleed or leave them to die at the hands of unimaginable monsters. I shook my head, doing the best I could to push those complex emotions aside for some time in the future, when I could eat a giant cupcake and down an entire bottle of wine from the comfort of my couch.

I held my spear ready despite my screaming ribs, but I didn't need to, not really. All the cultists had run or were down for the count in some other way. Harley was still engaged in her long-ass spell. I ran to check on Gareth and found his breath was shaky. It was still there, which was good, though he hadn't regained consciousness.

I yelled to Harley, "Gareth's down! We need to make this quick."

Harley gritted her teeth through whatever she was experiencing, and she paused long enough to shake her head before continuing. The spell would take as long as it would take. She needed an immense amount of power to take down the structure, to leech the magic out of the wood to ground it, which would help destroy it, and as good as she was, she didn't have enough magic to get through the process quickly. I didn't know enough to give her my magic, and I doubted it would be enough either. Not enough to make sure Gareth was safe and healed and this entire black church business was finished once and for all. Though, I knew something was here that was more than enough. If he would agree to help.

Harley watched with wide eyes and a shaking head as I pushed through my pain and bolted behind the altar. I gave her a shrug, hoping she understood what I was trying to do, as I crouched through the small door, unchained and open to me, and saw what I knew I'd see: the small, iron spiral staircase leading up to the steeple.

I climbed as quickly as I could and shoved open the door to see the black lion in the flesh. It shook out its mane, tilted its head in acknowledgment, and stood to stretch out its front and back legs, as if it knew it was about to run free.

"Can you understand me?" I yelled at the beast.

It didn't talk back. It was a lion, after all. It did nod, as if it could understand what I said.

"You let me know how to free you, and I will. After I do, you have to help my friends downstairs. One needs a jolt of power to do a spell that will take this whole gross black church down. The other is hurt, and we need him functioning to help finish the job."

The lion stared, and its black eyes, a starless night in miniature, appeared fathomless and unknowable. I breathed deep, waiting for what felt like forever for some answer, when he nodded again. Turning as best he could to face me full on, he pawed and growled at the floor.

There was carpet stapled down, but I dug in with my spear, cutting a small slit so I could pull and dig with my hands. Under the cheap carpet and padding was some sort of sigil structure. Likely a circle of power. I had no time to figure out exactly what it was, but I knew one thing from my basic training: break the writing of a sigil or circle of power, break whatever work it did. I reared back and slammed the spear into the subfloor beneath, chipping away at the paint until a shockwave fluttered out. A large gouge ripped through the circle where I'd buried my spear, a scar large enough to break the sigil circle and its hold on the beast.

The black lion grumbled near, and I turned back to him. He pawed again, this time at his throat, and I noticed the cracked leather band there again. It was another circle of sigils, this time worked straight into the leather cord. I crawled forward and, as gently as I could, slipped the sharp edge of the spear between the lion's neck and the cord. It stood still and silent, waiting patiently. I pulled down carefully, and the band snapped in two, falling to the carpeted floor.

The lion backed up several paces, stretching its neck before it let loose a defiant roar. Not the roar of a lion—or any animal, really. The roar of something older than the stars, and more powerful. It made fear and hope run wild in my veins as the thrum of magic in my gut ratcheted up a notch, going into an even higher frequency. It was the roar from my first night here, but no longer filled with sadness. This was a roar of triumph.

The big cat trotted back to me, studied my face for a moment, and licked his rough tongue across my shoulders to taste my blood. Not the greatest thing, though at first I thought it was to heal me like he had with the splinter. Nope. Just tasting my blood, because I still had a gaping slash on me.

He shuddered, closed his eyes for a moment, and looked down at the floor. His body shook, and he purred. At first it was a soft sound, then it grew louder and louder until it filled every nook and cranny of the attic and the church below, until the entire space vibrated to his call. I felt the purr deep in my gut, and in other places I was not prepared to think about. It was magic, and power made sound, and it zinged through me, strengthening me. Somehow it healed my shoulder, sounding through flesh to heal bone, knitting together anything that wasn't whole in me.

Distantly, as the purr softened again, I heard Gareth cry out to Harley. Felt a blast of a different sort of power from below, and knew Harley and Gareth needed me there. The black lion had done his part. Time for me to let him go.

I reached up to pat his head, and he leaned into me, rubbing his massive muzzle across my hand and giving me a last taste. With a good-bye lick of his rough tongue, he trotted toward the steeple vents, leaped through, and disappeared into the night.

Twenty-Five

I HAD NO TIME to lose, so I scrambled out and down, blinking away my spear so I could run full tilt toward a huddled Harley and Gareth. I took a minute to check with DD, which felt whole and strong and right by my side, just as the thrum inside me felt connected and strong after encountering the black lion. I didn't have time to think on either besides doing the basic acknowledgment as I reached the mages.

"What have you done?" Harley asked, her voice tinged with an odd echo of power. Not the black lion's power but something all her own, gathered both from and for the spell.

"I got us the extra jolt of magic we needed," I said. "Let's get this over with."

Harley sighed but carried on with her work. She moved slightly away from us, lifting the circle of power to complete the last part of the spell. The floating ring surged away from her, going up into the rafters, and split down, drenching pieces of black wood inside the church in a shimmery blue light. There was a pulse, a flash, and suddenly, the church structure groaned and shuddered and heaved, as if in relief. Harley herself shimmered blue for a moment, a powerful mage standing tall and proud, filled with magic and purpose and power. It was an awesome sight, and if I'd had my phone, I would've snapped a pic to show Merry.

The glow dimmed, and she spoke, her voice losing most of the echo of power as she said, "It should be untethered now. Without magic and destructible." Harley looked at Gareth. "You good?"

"Yes. I can do what needs to be done," he answered, planting his feet firmly and drawing on a sigil somewhere currently not visible through his clothes. A flicker of gray flame burst onto his upturned palm. He moved gingerly to a pew, laid his palm down there, and the flame spread like a creeping vine, slowly but surely, moving from pew to pew, then reaching up the walls. Before it had grown too far up and over, he said, "It's done. We need to leave. Now."

We ran, though not too far. We stood fifty yards from the church, watching and waiting. Close enough to hear the cracking and groaning of wood. We watched as the church folded in on itself. This was no fire but a compression inward. The large black building became smaller, cracked, and crumbled into a gray mass of what looked like ash. It lost density and form, becoming dust. The wisps of what used to be wood floated away bit by bit until it blew out of existence in front of our eyes. All that remained was us, the clearing where the black church had once stood, and the shelter house below. It wasn't made from the same stuff, so we could deal with it later.

Harley bent over, putting her hands to her knees, and waited long moments before she said, "We took down the black church. We actually did it."

"Macy's gone too," I muttered.

Gareth looked at me and I shook my head, not wanting to talk about it just then.

"Lots scattered. Some might come back, try to rebuild, but they lost a lot of power tonight. I'd call it a win."

"For sure," I agreed.

"Are we not going to talk about the beast? The magical power surge? The healing?" Gareth asked.

"It can wait a few," Harley said with a flip of her hand before she flopped onto the grass on her ass. "We can rest, take the win, at least for now."

I nodded. I didn't want to think on all we'd have to discuss, all I'd have to process, shortly. We needed a breather. I slid down beside Harley, knocked my shoulder into hers because it was no longer injured, and sent her a wide grin. "How're we celebrating tonight?" I asked.

"What kind of cupcakes you got?"

"Didn't create a defeating-an-evil-cult recipe. I really should've, but no time. You'll have to settle for whatever I have left in stock."

"Will there be any chocolate?" she asked.

"Probably." I laughed before standing and offering her a hand. "Let's go see. Put Merry and Mia out of their misery too."

At the mention of Merry's name, Harley's eyes lightened, and I was happy to see it. She took the lead, heading to her car. Gareth and I walked a little more slowly behind her.

"You really good?" I whispered to him as I took his arm in mine.

"I'm really good. Are you?"

I thought about it. I wasn't exactly good. Too much had happened. Too much was still unknown. I answered honestly. "I'm okay, I think."

He nodded, pulling his arm from mine to give me a warm, calming sideways hug. "You'll get to good. I know it."

I wanted to believe him, so I decided I did and left it alone, walking side-by-side with Gareth in peaceful silence toward Harley's car and, eventually, Warm Regards and my sisters.

THE REUNION AT WARM Regards went about as expected. Merry fussed over me and Harley. She even fussed a little over Gareth despite not knowing him too well. Mia was snarky as usual, but the crease I'd thought were now permanently stamped on her forehead had eased when we walked through the door, and she gave me a long, hard hug before we could tell them what had gone down.

We sat in the kitchens for an hour, rehashing what had happened, thinking through anything we may have missed.

"I don't like..." Harley said, looking over at me.

"I know. I know. You're upset I freed the lion—the beast or whatever. It was the only way I knew to get you charged and make sure Gareth was okay. Could it bite us in the ass later? Sure. Am I sorry I did it? Not even a little."

Harley nodded in understanding. "It might not have been my choice, but it's understandable," she said. "We do, however, need to keep it in mind as we move forward."

"Move forward how? The cult is gone. The church vanished. Aren't we done? Or, at least, I'm done. Right?"

"Randy," Merry said, pulling away from Harley's side to give me a hug. "I think you know you can't be done."

I sagged. Merry was right. I knew all this stuff about the occult and magic and evil swirling. I had all this power I was just beginning to understand. There was no way I could stop and sleep at night. I wasn't one to ignore facts, but it'd been nice to dream about an end goal, a point when this would be over and I'd go back to business as usual, but business would never be usual for me.

"What's next?" I groused.

Harley straightened, grabbed Merry around the waist, and said, "Next is sleep. Rest. Keeping an eye out so we make sure those damn cultists don't pop up somewhere else." She eyed me. "You did well. More than well tonight. You still need practice and knowledge, but you have time now. Time to study and learn without Starry Wisdom trying to snatch you."

"We'll help," Gareth said, straightening himself.

"Of course we will," Harley replied, as if offended he'd suggest she wouldn't help. It made me grin, her gruff friendship. "Also, I think there was talk of a chocolate cupcake of some sort?"

As promised, I pulled out a cupcake for Harley. One for Gareth too. She'd wanted chocolate, and there was a mass of Buckeye cupcakes left for the next day. Swiping five wouldn't hurt business. The pillowy peanut butter frosting with a chocolate sauce drizzle topped a luscious dark-chocolate cake, I knew, would be moist and decadent. It always was. One reason it was a favorite for my customers. Plus, the all-things-Buckeyes attitude that dominated in Columbus.

Mia was already halfway through her cupcake when Harley took a tentative bite of her own. She smiled my way and raised it in the air, like she was toasting me with it. I'd take it, for sure, so I raised mine back.

Gareth caught on and did the same, saying, "To righting our world."

"At least a little," I added, a smile and peanut butter frosting on my lips. Both felt good after all we'd accomplished.

Twenty-Six

After we stuffed our faces with cupcakes, and maybe a cookie or two, we were about to say our good-byes for the night when a bell tinkled. It was weird because the only bell I had was the one over the front door of Warm Regards, and it would be firmly locked and bolted this late at night. All heads whipped around toward the sound, and a beat later, I ran toward the front of the cafe, DD shivering in anticipation at my side. I needed to see the source of the sound, because immediately after the sound had made its way to my ear, a now-somewhat-familiar power skittered across my skin, caused my thrum of magic to go haywire in my gut.

Harley and Gareth were close on my heels, though they made sure Merry and Mia were firmly behind them, protected by a wall of mages. It made my heart squeeze but only for a moment. Because what I saw made no actual sense.

It was the man of my vision at Heatwave. He was tall, his lean but defined muscles showing through an open, black leather jacket with no shirt underneath. His leather pants matched the jacket and molded beautifully to his hips and legs. Hair flopped in his face slightly, an odd quasi-eighties style that wasn't exactly in but looked good on him. He pulled his lusciously full lips back in a broad, open smile. His face was like an ancient statue made of flesh, all hard angles compiled into a rigid grace and beauty. Except for the sensuous curves of his mouth. And his eyes. His eyes were the same black, starless night as the lion trapped in the steeple, and I knew they were one and the same.

"My sweetling," he practically purred. "It is so very good to finally meet you in the flesh." He scented the air like an animal, like a lion, and sent a wink my way.

I turned back to my friends and family when Harley growled, and I watched as she shoved Merry more fully behind her and her defensive sigils glowed. Gareth's stance widened, his feet planted firmly in front of Mia, hiding her with his bulk. He was ready to fight. Merry and Mia looked a little scared, but they took their cues from me in the front, so curiosity was also clear on their faces. They wanted to know why I wasn't in defensive mode. Why I hadn't reacted the same way about the hot, leather-clad guy in my café long after closing.

I wasn't defensive because DD shook in my vision. I could call on it. I knew I could have the spear in my hand in moments. Create my bubble. Do whatever I wished. The thrum inside wanted something else, needed something else. DD also wasn't amped in the same way it had been at the church. It was doing its odd little happy dance.

I'd trusted my magic in our battle and it'd helped, so I stepped up, not with magic, only with myself. "Who are you?" I asked, the person's power still rolling over me, somehow energizing as it pounded into me.

"My apologies," he said and gave a sweep of his hand as he bowed. "I know all of you, but most of you have never seen me before." He winked at me, then continued. "They most often call me Nyarlathotep, the Prince of the Dreamlands, but my friends call me Ny. I'm here to help."

"Help with what?" Harley asked through clenched teeth.

"Your problem. My problem. Our common enemy, whoever it might be."

"What?" I asked, utterly confused. I thought we'd just fought our enemy. An enemy who worshipped this Outer God standing in my café.

"Starry Wisdom has been a bother for many years, but only because someone with power backs them."

"That's not you?" Mia asked with a snide tone as she hid behind Gareth's back. I whipped my head around to stare daggers at my little sister. Even if I wasn't freaked out by the guy, I didn't want my little sister getting snarky with a possible Outer God.

He chuckled at Mia's snarky outburst, the sound sending tingling zaps of energy down my spine. "They like to claim so, and who knows what the rank and file are told, but no. Not the leaders who pulled the strings. Hence the kidnapping and imprisonment. It's another god they serve who gives them power, but we need to figure out which one and why."

His voice was a proclamation, and the idea of another god somewhere out to get me didn't feel the best. A different kind of shiver raced through my body, and I knew whatever happened with the cult was about to ramp up in a not-so-fun way, and all things cult had been decidedly not-so-fun already.

Harley squinted back at the Outer God, defiant and in defensive posture still. "I don't trust you," she stated plainly, always honest.

He continued to smile. "Usually, it would be smart for you not to trust me. Here and now, I give my word you can. In this case. While we search out the real power behind the cult."

Gareth asked, "What does the word of an Outer God mean to mortals?"

The prince didn't look like he took offense exactly, but he also didn't appear okay with the continued questioning of his motives. I blinked at Gareth, wondering why he'd be so antagonistic toward a god being, when Nyarlathotep replied coolly, "More than you can fathom, young one."

I needed to step in before blood got all over my bakery display case. Turning to face Harley and Gareth, leaving my back to the god in our midst for emphasis,

I said, "Look. I feel like he's being honest. Like, as in, feel it in here." I thumped my chest for emphasis. "Same reason I felt he'd help us before." Looking between the two mages, I whispered, "Trust me and my power, even if you can't trust him."

Harley hesitated but gave a chin lift in agreement.

Gareth offered a small but tight smile and eased his stance to show he'd back me. I heard a coo from behind me.

"Thanks, sweetling. Your little speech makes me feel all special."

I whirled around to him. "Are you going to kill us?" I asked outright.

"No. I have no reason to kill anyone in this room."

"Good. Harley and Gareth, back down for now. I need a drink, and I guess we all have more to chat about, so let's go."

I was tired, tense, and worried. Even if no one else wanted one, I really needed a drink. The bar down the block was most definitely calling my name. We had more to consider, more to discuss, and now we had an Outer God chilling in my café, calling me pet names.

Merry had been right. I wasn't done. Not yet. Maybe not ever.

Want to hear what the Outer God has to say, and how
Randy reacts to it all?

Read Book 2, *Shadow in the Witch House*
Out April 14th, 2023

Want More?

Interested in what Nyarlathotep was up to before he walked into Warm Regards? Join my newsletter and get a (very steamy) prequel story featuring the Prince of the Dreamlands. Click here to download the free story.

You can also visit my website (sonyalawson.com) or follow me on social media (@sonyalawsonwrites on Facebook, Instagram, and TikTok) for more info about me and my books.

And don't forget to preorder Book 2, *Shadow in the Witch House*, on Amazon today!

Acknowledgments

As always, the fabulous editors at Novel Nurse Editing deserve all the praise for their keen eyes, sharp minds, and ready comments. Janna and Angie improve my work every single time and I can't thank them enough.

100 Covers did an amazing job with the cover art. So much so it helped cement a few ideas in the book, so thanks for that.

My ARC Team continues to grow, and I appreciate each one of them. As a group, they give thoughtful feedback on every book and hype me up like no one else. They're a great group of readers and general human beings who I can't thank enough.

In case you didn't know, Heatwave is an actual thing. You should check it out if you're ever in Columbus the first Saturday of any given month. It's a great dance party with inspired DJs. One of these DJs, Lady Sandoval, is a good friend. She and DJ Scoppa (who started the whole thing) gave me permission to use the dance party by name in a pivotal scene in the book. I love Lady Sandoval for many reasons, but she's owed a big thank you for helping me out with this. Miss you lots and hope I get to dance with you again soon!

The Wednesday Mastermind Group helped me with my tag lines, blurb, cover revisions, and a mass of other things. They've been a great source of knowledge, help, and friendship these past few months. Plus, they're fabulous people to spend an hour a week with, so that doesn't hurt. Thanks, all!

The RRA group chat is lively in all ways, but also helpful whenever I have questions or need to vent about writer business things, so a big hug and thanks go to them as well.

My husband gives me the space and support to do this writing thing even if it drives us both a little up the walls at times, so thanks for putting up with so much, Ario.

Finally, thanks go out to Columbus and all the friends I have there. I dropped into that city at a rough moment in my life. Seven years later, I left with friends who were like family, actual family, lots of funny stories, and a love for that odd little Midwestern city. I'm more than grateful for the people and places that made my life there beautiful.

About the Author

Sonya Lawson is a recovering academic currently writing steamy modern fantasy with maybe a few too many literary references. Her stories may differ, but they all have at least one common characteristic — sassy, intelligent women trying to do the best they can in whatever world they inhabit.

While she remains a rural Kentuckian at heart, she's spent a lot of time in the Midwest and currently lives in the Pacific Northwest. She fills her days with writing, editing, reading, walking through old forests, and watching sitcoms or horror films with her husband. Two rowdy cats terrorize her house regularly, but she loves it.

You can get more information about past books, current projects, and upcoming releases at www.sonyalawson.com.

Don't forget to follow her on all her socials to stay connected. Find her on TikTok, Instagram, and Facebook using her username @sonyalawsonwrites.

www.ingramcontent.com/pod-product-compliance
Lightning Source LLC
Chambersburg PA
CBHW021146310726

48971CB00002B/505